LAKE JUNE
LOST AMONG THIEVES, BOOK 1

by P.L. Stafford

GalBay
League City, Texas

GalBay, LLC
2925 Gulf Fwy S. Suite199
League City, TX, 77573

LAKE JUNE: Lost Among Thieves

ISBN: 978-1-7325583-1-1

Cover designed by Dynasty's Visionary Designs, Newark, NJ, USA

Dedicated to Lamonica, Lashanda and Mario

The three beautiful flowers that bloom in the middle of my oasis

CHAPTER ONE

Dallas, like every other city in America, has its good and bad parts. Tina grew up in a neighborhood that is arguably middle ground. It is the part where the good and bad often collide, and the haves and have-nots often clash. Called "P.G." by the kids, Pleasant Grove spans an area large enough to be a city in itself. It is one of the most diverse areas in the Metroplex housing every racial, social and economic group you can imagine. However, most of its residents have never been outside of the state of Texas except for the occasional trip to Oklahoma or Louisiana. Old fifties and sixties-era wood-framed homes line the narrow, pothole riddled asphalt roads. Yet, the kids can be seen throughout the day riding their bikes up and down them, or running about them playing hopscotch or some type of ball.

When it isn't too hot, or the threat of random gunfire is low, people will sit out on their porches and visit with their neighbors. There are oftentimes drunks, drug dealers, and prostitutes roaming about, and it is commonplace to be greeted at the neighborhood store by someone with a spray-bottle and newspaper offering to wipe down your windows in return for your spare change.

The main strip is called Lake June. It is here that everything goes down from drug deals to gang hits. The majority of the businesses on Lake June are extravagant, high-end and owned by criminals, trying to legitimize their excessive incomes. There are at least eight clubs, nine bars, seven restaurants and six detail shops within 12-block radius between Stanton and Cooper. Every other vehicle is a Cadillac or Chevrolet and state of the art stereo systems, elaborate paint jobs, and shiny wheels are not only common but also expected. The women that frequent these parts are likened to magazine-models, with pretty faces and beautiful bodies. Lake June is said to be like a store open twenty-four-seven, selling everything from ass to Zigzags. It's not a place for the weak or timid, or a place for the naïve. Everyone on Lake June is either hustling or being hustled.

Tina, short for Christina, is a Black-Hispanic whose family moved to the area long before she was born. She lived off Cooper Road, just two blocks south of Lake June.

When she was younger, she would occasionally walk to the corner store to buy cigarettes for her mom, and the men would approach her with questions like "Hey baby, what are you?" and she would cleverly respond, "Blessed," while walking away. Tina was born to a Mexican father and African-American mother and celebrated the customs and cultures of both. She was as proud to be Latino as she was to be Black, but normally gave little weight to the often-distracting issues of race. However, she was unquestionably intrigued by the guys who raced up and down Lake June in their lavish cars, and they were equally intrigued with her and her long legs and curvaceous body. She was tall for a girl at 5'9, with measurements of 36-24-38 and weighing a measly 149 pounds. Her eyes were light brown, and her lips were soft and evenly toned. She had curly black hair that extended down her back, and flawless caramel colored skin. Her walk was confident, sexy and alluring, but never distasteful. At nineteen, she was already built like a grown woman, and many men solicited her for relations. Yet, she had faithfully dated but one man, Ronald Thurgood, throughout her entire time in high school. She was well-liked back at her school being bilingual, a straight "A" student and member of the debate team. It seemed that a life of fairytale proportions was well within her grasp when she was nominated "Most Likely to Succeed" and the University of Texas awarded her a full ride academic scholarship. However, prior to realizing her immediate dreams, she met neighborhood thug, Jonathan Cain.

Jonathan, who was generally considered good-looking, was six feet tall and 220 pounds. He had a slightly muscular build and well-distinguished cheeks with deep-set dimples. His beard was low-cut and meticulously trimmed. He was always clean-cut and well dressed, and his manner was often polite and charming. However, he was not one to be taken lightly. This one was likened unto the devil's son and his seemingly pleasant appearance only served to deceive. He was a major player in the half crescent that spanned from Lake June Avenue to Martin Luther King Boulevard, and at one point ran eight crack houses before he abandoned half of them and added armed robbery to his resume.

Known on the streets as JC, Jonathan knew nearly every O.G. and gang leader in the Metroplex, and just about all of them owed him favors. He was one who remembered every face and recalled every detail. Yet, despite all his talents, his level of success at nineteen was, even to him, sometimes inconceivable.

They met on Friday night, as Tina and two girlfriends walked out of the movie theater. The parking lots were full of people walking to and from their cars when he pulled up to the curb in front of them.

He was in a shiny black 1964 Cadillac, which rolled on a set of chrome 30 spoke wire wheels. The top was down exposing the tightly stitched white interior that seemed to showcase its occupant, who wore a bright red shirt and a smile that could sell chitterlings to a Muslim. "Hello ladies," he said, as he laid his arm across the back of the passenger seat, and simultaneously pressed a solenoid that made the passenger door swing open as if an invisible valet had done it. "Would you like to go for a ride?" he said in a confident baritone voice that seemed to pierce the veils of their inner beings. "Yeah!" both of Tina's friends yelled at once, as they jumped into his car. However, after noticing that Tina neither moved nor replied, he stepped out of the car and approached her. Grabbing her hand and gently raising it to his chest, he kissed it and kindly asked her to come. But, she again refused.

Then, in response to the challenge, JC spent the next 30 minutes talking with her on a bench near the theater's entrance. Moments after they sat down, she noticed a man in the background placing two large bags in JC's trunk, but made no mention of it. She was impressed with his level of conversation and confidence, and played careful attention to the way he handled the frequent interruptions of her friends and cleverly drew everyone's attention away from the activities in the background. He had been extremely charming and entertaining, and both of Tina's friends were smitten. The looks they gave him were that of hungry vultures eyeing the inviting feast of fresh road kill. They hung on his every word. Then, just as unexpected as his arrival, was his sudden departure.

"Well, I must be going," he said, "but if you ever want to taste the greatest steaks in the Metroplex, try Xavier's on Lake June. Give the waiter this card and they'll place the meal on my tab. Have a nice evening, ladies." And like a brisk breeze, he had almost in one continuous motion, moved from the bench to the car and only the cranking of the engine broke the power of his spell. Vroom! The engine roared at the turning of the key, and JC inched away under the amplified sound of Africa Bambaataa's "Planet Rock."

Tina smiled as she looked down at the card, and one of her friends screamed, "Girl you better get you some of that. That boy's fine!"

"Na," Tina replied, "he's not really my type."

"...Your type? Then what the hell's your type?"

"Don't know, but it ain't that."

"You're tripping girl...Let's go..."

The three of them laughed as they began to walk towards Tina's car. They were stopped three or four times by men who were trying to come on to them, but this was typical for this area and for these girls: all tall, beautiful, and built like goddesses. They joked amongst themselves as they continued on. They had parked pretty far away because it was opening night for Steven Spielberg's E.T.: The Extra-Terrestrial and the parking lots were nearly full when they arrived. Yet, hidden in the sea of cars and people, appeared Tina's multicolored 1968 Impala: a car that had spent its fourteen-year life in the hands of inexperienced drivers and had the battle wounds to prove it. Even so, they got in one by one: loading from the passenger's side because the driver's side door was jammed. They slid across what was left of the old vinyl seats, stepped over a few exposed wires, and with a couple of cranks and a cloud of black smoke, managed to get it started. Tina then turned on the radio, and the sounds of the local radio station barely pierced through the engine interference, but after pushing a tape in the deck, Kool & the Gang's "Celebration" rang loudly through the one working speaker.

Approximately forty-five minutes after his encounter with Tina, JC pulled into an alley behind one of Lake June's premier nightclubs, Crimson Moon. This was an establishment with humble beginnings, to say the least. It began as an old warehouse that had offices situated on its upper two levels. However, JC acquired it from a client whose habits exceeded his ability to pay, and after throwing three or four big parties inside it, he decided to convert it into a club.

As he pulled up to the loading dock, you could hear the sound of music playing inside. A large metal door swung open, and he drove inside and parked between a bright-silver Mercedes and a dark blue Suburban.

He was met by a man who was tattooed from head to toe. He was 6'1 and completely bald, except for a goatee that hung three inches below his chin. He had on black slacks and a navy blue Ban-Lon shirt that displayed the results of hours in somebody's gym. He wasn't exactly Hercules, but he was ripped like he hadn't eaten in weeks.

"What's up, bro?" He greeted JC with an elaborate handshake and hug that only close acquaintances would recognize or allow.

"What's up, Deuce? You got my stuff?"

"Have I ever not had your stuff?"

"No, and you better not, never not have my stuff, neither."

"...Whateva, nigga."

"Yea, whatever," JC scoffed, "...where's my stuff?"

Deuce, of course, wasn't too fond of being talked down to, but such back and forth banter was common between the two of them, and since JC was his meal ticket, he often had to swallow it in the end. Nevertheless, Deuce nodded and handed him a black garment bag. JC reached inside it and pulled out a blue blazer that matched the pants he was wearing. After putting it on, he reset his collar and looked back at Deuce.

"Where's your jacket?" JC uttered.

Deuce reached over to the chair where he had been sitting and grabbed the jacket that was draped over it.

"Why we gotta dress up for this sissy anyway? Hell, a brother's the same brother whether he's in a suit or jeans, so he may as well be comfortable."

JC didn't even honor him with a reply. He just grabbed the bags from the trunk of the Cadillac and placed them in the trunk of the Benz.

You see, JC and Deuce were not exactly friends. They were partners in crime. JC had done some unmentionables in the past, and Deuce had proven to be resourceful, so JC shot him a gig here and there when it suited him. However, Deuce's primary importance to JC relied on his management of JC's street interests and his knowledge of bank and armored car invasions. Deuce, on the other hand, knew that JC was involved in a lot more than he ever mentioned and wanted a piece of the action. However, his tendency to be impulsive and reckless made JC inclined to use him only when absolutely necessary. Other times, Deuce was simply company in a world where friends were few.

The two of them hopped into the Benz, and Deuce cranked the engine. The sound from the rear speakers rang so loud that the windows vibrated in their seals.

JC looked over and shouted, "Man, turn that shit down! —and

don't give them po-pos a reason to pull us over."

Deuce replied with his usual sarcasm, "Man, this my shit and Dick Tracy better stay his ass in the '50's." JC laughed as he reached for the volume knob, and turned the music down.

"You're ignorant you know that? Ignorant as the day is long." Deuce laughed at JC's comment and slowly backed down the dock.

They pulled around front, and JC rolled down the heavily tinted window and uttered to a valet "Have Betty gassed and gleamed and dropped off at the house." "Ok!" the valet replied as he caught the keys JC tossed to him.

JC had the valet take his plush 1964 Cadillac for a fill-up and detail to throw off any trailers and to ensure that it always appeared freshly detailed. "Let's do this," JC said to Deuce as he let up the window and the two of them drove off to meet Antonio.

It was about 8:30 when they arrived at Pelican Bay, a fancy restaurant owned by self-proclaimed, legitimate businessman, Antonio Ruiz. Deuce pulled up into the handicap parking across from the front entrance, and took a handicap tag from the glove box and hung it on the rearview mirror. They both chuckled and without a word being spoken, stepped out the car like two mafia hit men. There were two guys standing outside the entrance talking about the State Fair Classic. JC and Deuce walked past them and into the foyer, where a Latin woman stood in a fancy blue dress. She had long brown hair that was tied up in a ponytail and small oval glasses that hung low on her nose. She looked up at them, as they entered, and said, "Hello gentleman, do you have a reservation?" Deuce leaned over to reply, but JC placed his hand on Deuce's shoulder and said, "Si senorita, numero trece." She smiled and gleamed into his eyes for a second, and then looked down at the list. "Number 13, Alfonso Estabane," she said as she looked up and gazed deep into his eyes again. "Follow me to your table, please."

As she walked them along a long peach-colored wall and up a narrow stairwell, Deuce whispered to JC, "Who the hell are you again?" JC just smiled as he looked back down the stairs. The two men from the parking lot were following close behind. They were obviously friends of Antonio's and only there to ensure that things remained in order. There were more men standing at the top of the staircase, and the anxiety in the room was high.

JC looked across the room and saw a man gagged and tied up with strips of thinly cut linen. He had been beaten up pretty badly and was bleeding profusely. JC had seen him on the streets before. He was one of them who had agreed to work for Antonio only to find out the hard way, that the devil makes no square deals.

JC looked up from him just in time to catch Antonio's entrance. He wore an expensive blue Italian suit and a plum-colored shirt with a large butterfly collar. He had bushy eyebrows and one of those haircuts that were designed to look messed up. His mustache covered his top lip almost completely. He was a tall, heavyset man who walked with a slight limp for whatever reason and was focused on JC from the moment he entered the room. His smile was malicious and mischievous at once.

"Jonathan!" he said with the raspiest Colombian voice ever spoken. "You ready to come work for me?"

"Na, I gave up on Corporate America long ago," JC said, and everyone laughed.

"Who's your friend, JC?"

"This is Deuce, from California."

"California, huh? He looks like a cop."

"Come on Antonio," JC chuckled, "Deuce is no cop."

"Yeah? Well, I don't like him. Get rid of him."

Just then, two men grabbed Deuce, but he snatched loose and yelled, "What's up?" Yet, before he could await an answer, he had been snatched away and thrown down the stairs. Deuce slowly got up and noticed one of the parking lot guys standing over him with a gun to his head. "Walk away, brother. Just walk away," the guy said, as he stepped back and placed the gun back in the holster beneath his jacket. Deuce stood up and straightened his jacket, and without a hint of a warning delivered a Tyson type punch. Parking lot boy was out cold. Deuce took his gun and the cash from his wallet. "Yeah, I'll walk off, walk off with some moolah," he said, as he stepped out of the stairwell into the dining room and headed for the front door. It was still business hours, so little was likely to happen to him outside in front of the customers. Meanwhile, JC and Antonio had words upstairs, and JC didn't come down for another fifteen minutes. When he finally arrived at the car, he found Deuce leaning against the passenger door with a gun in his hand.

"We have to come back in an hour," JC said.

"For what?"

"To finish the deal."

"For what?"

"What the hell you mean, for what?"

"He's got the stuff right there. He ain't gotta go nowhere and get it. Pedro, José, Raymond and 'nem high as hell and he's gonna throw me down a flight 'o mutherfuckin stairs...I'm going back up there."

"Get in the car, Deuce," JC interrupted.

"Get in the car? Man, I told you, this my shit. You get in the mutherfuckin car." Chirp! Chirp! JC smirks as he climbed into the car and turned the radio knob to the off position before Deuce could get around to the driver's side and get in.

"So what we s'posed to do for an hour, J?"

"I don't know. Let's go to Johnnies and play a quick game of pool."

"Cool, a place where there're some black people."

JC laughed and replied, "Yeah, and no stairs for you to be thrown down."

It was five minutes after nine when they arrived at Johnnie's, and John-boy had a full house.

"JC!" screamed a familiar voice from across the room. He glanced past him as if he didn't see him and placed an order at the bar. The skinniest man living then walked up to him trying to adjust the twice broken and taped coke bottles he called glasses.

"JC! JC! I got him," he said anxiously. "That contact you been asking 'bout. I got him."

"Have him meet me tomorrow at six pm ...Crimson Moon."

"Ok, ok JC," he replied, with his hand stuck out awaiting payment for his task. JC put Deuce's beer in his hand and said, "I'll pay you once I know he's the right guy." Almost immediately, Deuce snatched the beer back from him and downed it in one swallow.

"My brother," Deuce shouted, and then followed with a huge burp, Urrrrrrr! "Ain't shit in life free."

JC just smiled and looked over at table number seven, the hustler's table. Everyone was standing around watching two women run the pool table.

"What they hitting for?" JC asked a bystander.

"Two-hundred a game."

"Two-hundred?"

"Yeah, and they 'bout $1,800 up."

JC smiled as the girls went up $2,000 and motioned for their next challenger. Yet, no one moved. Everyone had either already been taken or was just enjoying the site of them bending over. However, this was JC's game. He grabbed a cue from the rack and checked it for straightness.

The tall woman yelled over, "You have two-hundred to lose?"

"No I don't," JC said, "but if you up the ante to $2,000, I would be glad to oblige."

The crowd urged on in response to the offer, and the girls discussed this briefly amongst themselves and gladly accepted the wager.

"So we playing head up or what?" said the shorter woman, as she stood with one hand on her hip and the other on her cue.

"Heads up is fine," JC said, "So who will I be playing, you?"

"Of course," she replied, as she placed the triangle on the table and yelled, "Rack 'em!"

She was about 5'5 with a bust and booty too large for her small frame. When she leaned over for the break, everyone in the room leaned over with her. A little guy at a nearby table had a fix on her breast like a cheetah on a baby gazelle. If one of them had managed to pop out, he definitely would've got a case. "*HORNY MAN MAULS WOMAN AT LOCAL BAR*" the papers would read.

They went back and forth dropping balls and quasi-sexual comments as they played. JC looked down at his watch and determined that fun time was over, and with every trick shot in the book, cleared the table, and honed in on the eight ball. "This is for you, my love, eight-ball in the corner pocket." And with one smooth stroke, the game was done.

The girl handed the money to JC, but when he took hold of it, she attempted to snatch it back. "Double or nothing," she said, but he refused.

"I have somewhere to be, maybe next time," he replied.

"Won't you give me a chance to redeem myself?" she said, still holding firm to the money.

"No!"

"Hey! I can't afford to lose this money. Just play it back. One more game!" she yelled.

"Look, you knew when we racked 'em that you could leave here broke, but greed forced you to grow balls you didn't have. Now, let go."

Refusing to accept her failure, the woman snatched away from JC and the money flew out of their hands and fell to the floor.

"I want a rematch, damn it!" she screamed in a way that silenced the entire bar.

"Okay! Okay, wait a minute," said Deuce, who suddenly interceded. "You know you hustled her anyway, JC. You don't need the money. Maybe we can let her keep it in exchange for a 'lil show-n-tell."

"Deuce..." JC motioned but was abruptly cut off by him.

"Fuck that! Let this desperate broad have the money, but make her show us them tits before she takes it."

JC felt the hairs stand on the back of his neck. He cut his eyes at Deuce and then back at the woman, looked her up and down as she had done him, forced a smile and then replied, "Ok, Ms. Thang, what'll it be, the tits or the money?" Knowing she lost fair and square and had no real rights to the money, she closed her eyes, rocked her head from side to side, and reluctantly lifted her shirt and let her luscious melons fall. The place was in an uproar. People stood up, clapped, whistled and screamed like the New Years Eve ball had just dropped in Times Square.

JC, again, looked down at his watch and then back at Deuce. "Come on. Let's go. It's 'bout that time." Deuce downed the remains of his beer and headed out to the car behind his partner in crime. However, as they exited the front door, JC suddenly turned around and drew down on Deuce.

"Damn, Nigga. What's up with this?" Deuce uttered as JC stepped closer, revealing a second gun from behind his back. Deuce froze. JC looked deep into his eyes as he approached, stopped just before him and broke a sudden smile.

"You ready to get paid, Nigga?"

"Hell, yeah!" Deuce replied as he handed him the second gun. "I thought your crazy ass had flipped out," Deuce continued, as they entered the car. However, when he reached for his seat belt, JC slammed Deuce's head against the window and placed the cold blue steel of his 9mm pistol to his temple. "Deuce," JC whispered, "as long as there's a God in heaven and air on earth for your punk ass to breathe; don't you ever mess off my money for a broad. I don't care if she has three titties and a pussy deep as the Atlantic, if you cross that line again, I will kill you where you stand. Now, get your ass together so we can do this."

Antonio was only ten minutes away, but it must have seemed like an hour because the car was dead silent. Not a word was spoken or a glimpse in the direction of the other. Guns within everyone's reach and $100,000 in the trunk, things could have easily gone bad. However, Deuce somewhat understood what JC meant, even though he disagreed with his manner. The incident played over and over in Deuce's head, and he thought to himself, if the shoe was on the other foot and he was JC, the results would have been the same, except he would have pulled the trigger. This made him break out a small chuckle.

"What's funny," JC asked.

"Did you see the nipples on that broad?" Deuce replied, and they both broke a smile and laughed.

"Yeah, they were huge, like a stack of dimes." More laughter followed and then things were silent again.

They arrived at Pelican Bay at 10:12 and JC advised him to drive around back. There was a large truck parked in the alley, but no one appeared to be inside, so Deuce pulled alongside it and popped the trunk.

"You sure you wanna do this alone?" he asked, and JC nodded yes.

After exiting the car, JC grabbed the bags, threw them over his shoulder, and advised Deuce to keep his eyes open.

"A'ight," Deuce replied, "I'll whip the car around and wait for you to come back. If you ain't back in five minutes, I'll call 911."

JC smiled and said, "Yeah, and when they show up, we'll tell 'em it's all your shit."

Deuce stepped back and watched him now walk up the stairs and knock on the door. His knocks were rhythmic as if it were some type of code. Yet, no one answered. Once again JC knocked. Knock! Knock! Nick! Knock! Knock! And, again, nothing happened until he turned and headed back down the stairs, a broad beam of light shot past him and illuminated the ground before him as the Metal door inched open. "You're late JC," said Eduardo, one of Antonio's top go-to men. No one knew Eduardo's last name. He was simply called 'Wardo on the streets. He was a couple of years older than JC but similarly minded, except for where 'Wardo was inclined to work for Antonio, JC wasn't. '

Wardo was a big guy who towered over JC some four or five inches and was probably twice as wide. He almost looked black, with his low cut wavy hair and broad nose, but he was Columbian and likely kin to Antonio. He stood at the door with his jacket half-opened so that the gun could be seen resting in its holster and motioned for JC to come in. As they stepped inside 'Wardo shut the door and told him to drop the bags. JC laid the bags on the floor, and another one of Antonio's men grabbed them, opened them, and looked inside. "How you get this?" he asked, but JC looked on without replying.

"Ok, up the stairs," 'Wardo interceded, as he pulled his gun from the holster and marched JC up the grey metal stairs to Antonio's private dining area.

"Sit!" Antonio uttered as JC entered the room. Mmm "This is the best damn steak I've ever had, and you know where I got it, JC?"

"...From your kitchen downstairs?" JC offered.

"No, from that shoddy restaurant of yours, Xavier's on Lake June. If it wasn't for you, I think I would have the chef killed, unless of course, he would work for me." He took another bite and shook his head agreeably and put down his knife and fork. JC was seated across from him like a kid about to be lectured by his father. Antonio looked deeply into his eyes and studied him.

"How's your mother, Jonathan?"

"She's fine. What's it to you?"

"...Just making small talk. That's what's wrong with this stinkin' generation. They have no place for pleasantries."

"Antonio, I just want to get my stuff and go."

"Yeah, yeah ...your stuff," he chuckled, as he wiped his mouth with a peach-colored napkin and rose from his chair. You've done well for yourself Jonathan: two car washes, a restaurant, a club and a budding Real Estate venture, and you're what, twenty?"

"I'm nineteen."

"Nineteen? Ahhh. Even better. And all this for what, Jonathan, to hide what you really do? Steal? You steal business from me. You steal business from others. You steal away my patience Jonathan, but me glad you intercepted that shipment them cock-a-roaches were trying to move through my city, cause they stealing from me, too. However, the truck you intercepted the other day and that facility you robbed, that too was mine. So as I see it, I owe you nothing. You owe me. I estimate you set me back 'o $200,000." JC jumped up from his seat to protest, and guns rose all over the room. Antonio motioned for his men to put their guns down and JC vigilantly continued.

"That wanna-be crack house only had $3,000 in it and less than a pound of weed...and that truck wasn't yours, it was Victor's, and it only had $35,000 and a bunch of meat!"

"No JC. Victor works for me, and as I told you, you owe me another $100,000, and I want it in a week." Antonio then grinned at him, like a man grins when he sees a woman he likes, and patted him on the cheek two times. "Get me my money," he whispered, as he stepped away and walked back to the head of the table. "Oh, by the way, JC," Antonio continued while seating himself and picking up his knife and fork. "I checked on your friend, Dos, and you're right. He's no cop. He's a maggot thief like you."

Everyone laughed as JC was walked out of the room, and continuously pushed and harassed on the way back to the rear door. Just as the door was opened, 'Wardo kicked JC in the back, and he fell down the steps. The door slammed shut behind him, and the sound of laughter was heard fading away from the other side of the door. Deuce walked over to JC with his head half-cocked to one side and helped him from the ground.

"You're empty-handed," he said.

"Yeah," JC replied, "the price just went up,"

The ride home was nearly as quiet as the ride there, minus the details of the night's events. Deuce pulled up to JC's place and drew a pint of gin out from beneath the seat. "

You may as well have a drink with a nigga."

"Nah, JC replied, "I'll catch you in the morning."

"A'ight, man. Don't come by my place before twelve," Deuce uttered while backing out the driveway. "...I'll shoot ya ass straight through the door. Pow! Pow! ...and think nothing of it."

Deuce downed the gin on the way to Lake June and decided to stop at a bootleg and get another. However, he arrived just in time to see Sam being escorted from his home by the police. "Po-pos," he muttered, as he passed with his window down and music playing loudly. One of the policemen walked toward the car and motioned for him to stop, but he kept going. He turned right at the corner and made it a couple of blocks before a police car sped up behind him. Wurp Wurp. The police siren chirped as the lights came on. Deuce slowed down, lowered the volume, and stopped under a light post adjacent to an apartment complex. He felt the police were less likely to misbehave in a place where there could be roaming eyes and people dying to testify of what they saw.

The police officer didn't get out the car immediately. He stayed put and waited for backup. Three other patrols showed up before the original officer walked over to Deuce and asked for his driver's license and insurance. Deuce took his driver's license out of his wallet and the insurance card from the glove department and handed them to him. The officer returned after ten minutes and asked Deuce to step out of the car.

"What's seems to be the problem, officer?" Deuce

responded, in a somewhat intellectual tone.

"Didn't you see the officer pulling you over back there?" said the officer, with a severely agitated look on his face.

"No, I'm sorry, I didn't. I was somewhat overwhelmed with all the lights," Deuce said with a smile. "I'm a real-estate investor looking at potential multifamily real-estate properties…"

"Shut up!" The officer interrupted, "We know who you are." Deuce chuckled and replied, "I beg your pardon…" "Shut up!" the officer yelled as he raised his finger to Deuce's face. "One day you'll slip up, and we'll have enough to put your ass away, or just maybe, we'll get lucky enough to shoot your ass in the streets."

"Dang," Deuce replied, "Why you gotta be like that?"

The officer snickered and stepped away from Deuce.

"You have a nice day, Mr. Smith," he said as he lowered his finger and walked back to his car.

"Chump," Deuce said as he grabbed his crotch and walked back to his car. Still holding his crotch, he stood inside the door and looked back at the officer and after a three-second pause got back into the car.

He grabbed the pistol from between the seats, placed it in his lap, turned up his music and drove off. One of the officers tailed him for a while, so Deuce passed on stopping at another bootleg. Instead, he headed on to Lake June and stopped at Caribbean Nites Bar & Grill. The painted yellow brick building had scenes from the Caribbean painted along its walls. The grass around it was more than ankle high, the music played loudly on multiple house speakers, and the smell of Jamaican love was in the air.

Deuce walked in and was greeted by a long-haired Rasta and escorted to his seat. He ordered jerk chicken and a beer. He stopped there every now and then to get away from the fast pace of his lifestyle. Caribbean Nites had good food and a laid-back atmosphere. It was a type of demilitarized zone where you checked your grudges and grievances at the door, had a good time, and picked up your belongings on the way out. It had that at home at momma's feel to it. The tables were hardwood and covered with red tablecloths. The chairs were old but sturdy. The floor was uneven in spots, but the table legs had been shaved to compensate. The rafters had exposed wood, and the support beams were bare as well. The light was used sparingly. It appeared almost exclusively at the bar, around the restrooms, pool tables, and cash register. You could be five feet from your worst enemy and not even see them.

Deuce was elbow deep in his chicken when he noticed dime stacks across the room at the pool table. She had stepped into the light just long enough for him to recognize her. She was watching her girl play pool. She was beautiful as he remembered: 5'5 with thunder thighs, store-bought curly hair, silky soft mocha skin, and big tits. They were running the same hustle they were at Johnnie's, but at one hundred a game this time. He made his way over to her and grabbed her from behind.

"Tit-o-biggy! What you doing?" he uttered.

"I'm minding my own business," she replied as she jerked away. However, Deuce just stood there for a minute and stared her down like a lion getting ready to pounce. She glanced back at him as if to say, he'd better not.

"You want a beer?" he asked.

"I'd like a Cosmopolitan."

"I said do you want a beer?"

"...excuse me! Who you think you are?" she sneered with aggravation in her voice, but Deuce just stood there watching her. "What!" she yelled. "Why are you just staring at me?"

"I'm deciding whether or not I'm gonna let you fuck."

"What?" she replied?

"You know ...whether or not I'm gonna let you sit on my dick." She laughed and shook her head from side to side. "Last time you did that you showed me your tits. What are you gonna show me now?"

She laughed some more.

"Nothing...You're the guy from the other place, huh?"

"Yeah, what's your name?"

"What's *your* name?"

"Deuce. Look, my foods getting cold. You gonna come over here and talk to me or what?"

"Ask me nicely."

"Okay. You gonna come over here and talk with me or what?" She smiled as if she was flattered by his response, and walked with him to his table. She sat down across from him and ordered the same thing he did. Their witty back and forth banter continued for another hour and a half before Deuce and dime-stacks found themselves kissing, hugging, and half-naked in the club.

"I'm 'bout to be out," Deuce said, "You coming with me or what?"

"Yeah," she replied as she pushed her breasts back into place and straightened her dress. "Let me tell my girl."

"Do dat," Deuce replied with a devilish look on his face. "I'm gonna tear her ass up," he mumbled as he walked up to the register and paid their tab.

She jumped into the car with Deuce and smiled. "My name is Christy." He looked over at her, nodded his head and then turned on the music. "This is a nice car," she said, but Deuce again just nodded. "So, where we going?" Deuce fired up a cigarette and simply stared ahead. "You don't talk much do you?" she continued.

"You don't shut up much either do you?" Deuce replied.

They arrived at his place, and she began to talk about her life and how everything had fallen apart or was outside of her immediate grasp. Deuce made simple interjections here and there, but mainly just listened and kept her glass full. After several hours of weed and wine, Deuce spread her apart and penetrated her love. She embraced him tightly as he stroked her. Several times a tear fell as she was brought to a raging climax, and the night ended with the two of them falling asleep in each other arms.

CHAPTER TWO

Honk! Honk! "What's that sound?" Deuce uttered softly while shielding the invading beam of light from the morning sun. Honk! Honkkk! "Who the hell's honking that horn?" he yelled, rubbing his eyes and pushing an empty bottle of Courvoisier out of the bed. Honk! Honnnkkkk! "Ok!" Deuce yelled as he grabbed his gun and reached for his boxers.

"What's going on, baby?" Christy asked, and Deuce's eyes quickly bucked like the cheeks of a blowfish."

"What the... Get up!" Deuce yelled as he grabbed her by the arm and dragged her out the bed.

"Baby?"

"Shut up and get your stuff!" he yelled as he placed the gun on the dresser, quickly slid on his jeans and grabbed the gun again. Christy was pulling her dress over her head when he grabbed her arm and dragged her out the front door.

"I said don't come by my place before 12." Pow! Pow! Deuce shot up into the air and paced back and forth in the yard. JC laughed and got out of the truck and walked over to Christy.

"Get in the truck and put on your clothes," he advised, as the neighbors stood around watching the show. Laughing almost uncontrollably, JC walked over to a seemingly panicking Deuce.

"I see you went back for dime stacks."

"Yeah," Deuce said while still pacing back and forth to complete the act, "and she got some good ass pussy too."

"So why you giving her the crazy-man act?"

"...Because I was drunk and brought her to my house. I should've taken her to a motel. What time is it? I said don't come by before twelve!"

"It's two o'clock, Deuce."

"Really?"

"Yeah."

"Man, I said don't come to my place before twelve!" Deuce yelled while trying to hold his smile.

"Crazy ass..." JC accused. "I'll take her home. Meet me at Crimson at 3:30."

"Yeah, Man. Take the scenic route so that broad don't remember where I stay."

"Yeah, Man, 3:30 ...white-folks time."

"What that mean?"

"That means don't be late."

"Forget you," Deuce said, as he dropped his act and walked into the house.

JC then left with the dirty work, walked back to the truck and leaned against the door where a shaken up Christy sat. "I'll take you home for two-thousand dollars," he said with a smile.

That afternoon, Deuce arrived at Crimson Moon at 3:45 p.m. The business lights were on but the doors were locked. He saw several vehicles in the parking lot, so he knew something was happening. He got on the phone and called JC, but he didn't answer. He called and paged everyone he could think of, the owners of the cars parked out front, the manager of Crimson Moon and Xavier's. Yet, no one answered.

He then laid back in the seat of his car listening to music and eventually fell asleep. He woke up two hours later to the sounds of cranking cars. He jumped out of his car and walked over to JC, who was speaking to one of the workers.

"What's up?" he said to JC as he approached. "What I miss?"

"Nothing."

"Nothing? Man, brotha's don't lock people outside for 'nothing'."

"No! Brotha's who are serious 'bout their paper don't find themselves locked outside for 'nothing'."

"Ok man," Deuce chuckled, "I was wrong. Now, what's up?"

"Nothing. I'll call you if I need you," JC replied, as he stepped back inside and closed the door behind him. Deuce, displeased with his answer, realized that there was no reasoning with him now, because he was in business mode, paper mode, as he would call it: a mode where everything is business, and nothing is personal, where words like family, friend and foe could change meanings in a matter of moments. It was this mode where JC was the most dangerous and unpredictable, and consequently, most effective. Yet, almost as soon as the door had closed, he had reopened it with a cordless phone held to his ear. He looked past the departing Deuce to two approaching gentlemen. Each looked as if they were from a place where dressing like nerds was cool. Even in the extreme Dallas heat, they both wore woven blazers, geeky pinstriped neckties and loafers that had weird looking tassels on them. Each of them wore glasses. One of them was tall and skinny and the other short and chubby.

"Hello Mr. Cain," the tall guy said, as he reached to shake JC's hand.

"Hello Mr. Abernathy," he replied as he shook their hands and invited them in.

"This is my good friend Bill, Bill Washington..." Mr. Abernathy continued, as JC closed the door behind them. "He knows everything there is to know 'bout electronics. I tell ya, he's 'bout sharp as they come. If the two of us cannot build what you need, then by gosh, it can't be done."

"Well gentlemen, I do appreciate you taking this meeting on such short notice, but I have a matter before me the needs immediate attention. If you have a seat at the table here, I'll tell you what we need." Everyone sat down and a young lady from Xavier's served snacks and refreshments. JC introduced himself as head of security for Crimson Moon. He said they had problems with electronic interference and believed the incoming signals were generated by competing clubs.

"What would they gain from such a thing?" Mr. Washington asked.

"People pay a lot of money to come to a club such as this to watch sports events, socialize with coworkers, blow off steam and find potential mates," JC replied. "When things don't work properly, customers tend to go elsewhere. Likewise, when our security officers can't communicate, they cannot control the people effectively when emergencies occur. What we need is a jamming device that would jam their signals and..."

"Why don't you just use shielded wiring?" Mr. Washington interjected. "It would be far more practical and economical."

"Yes, sir, but what we need is a jammer," JC continued while laying out the specs for his device. The meeting continued for another half-hour with JC selling his idea. Here and there, the men would interject and correct him on the finer points of their craft. However, there came a point when Mr. Abernathy became too uncomfortable to continue.

"Mr. Cain," Mr. Abernathy hesitated, "I apologize for being rude, but this is outright illegal, and the thought of it doesn't sit well with me. I don't know why you need such a device, but it's clear that you are not being honest with us."

"Maybe I am. Maybe I'm not," JC said, as a stress line appeared on his forehead, "but you're not here because you're patriots of legalism, Mr. Abernathy, but because you are patriots of self-preservation. You're here because a skinny man in broken glasses told you that you can make a quick tax-free $20,000. To what end the device is ultimately used is not your concern. Whether or not you can, and do, make it is your concern. So I ask you, gentlemen, can it be done?"

"...Well, I believe this meeting is done, Mr. Cain," Mr. Abernathy said as he wiped his forehead with a handkerchief. JC leaned back in his seat and watched Mr. Abernathy finish his lemonade. His hand shook so profusely it's amazing nothing spilled. JC looked at Mr. Washington who appeared equally uncomfortable.

"Can it be done, Mr. Washington?" JC reiterated

"We must go," Mr. Abernathy said as he hurried up from his seat patting his face profusely. Mr. Washington never looked up and never replied. He just stared at the tablecloth like he was wigging out on PCP. JC then rose to his feet, adjusted his jacket, and thanked them both for coming.

While escorting them to the door, JC sees Mr. Washington slide a card onto a table as he passed. There were the normal salutations that come with business conclusions, and the men departed.

JC returned to the table where Mr. Washington had left his business card. It had Washington Radio Products printed on the front, and $50,000 hand-written on the back. He smiled as he put the card in his coat pocket. "Phase one," he said aloud.

Feeling somewhat fatigued, JC called Greg, the club manager, from the back office and went over a few business concerns. He told him he was too tired to go over the books with him at the time, but would meet with him later in the week. The two of them shook hands and JC walked out to his Suburban. After he had climbed in, he rested his head on the steering wheel. It was 7:00 pm on a Saturday: a time where everyone was polishing their cars, preparing their outfits, and cleaning up for the upcoming night. In less than two hours there would be a line around the building and three different kinds of music blasting from Crimson Moon, but all he could think of was food, sleep, and the $100,000 he owed Antonio.

Beeeep! Beeeep! Beeeep! His pager went off. Beeeep! Beeeep! He grabbed it and looked at the display. It showed, "535537834" which read "HE BLESSES" when turned upside down. This was his mother's code, but he decided to stop by her house on his way home, rather than walking back into the club and calling her. She paged one more time while he was on the freeway.

He arrived at his mother's house at 7:30 and carefully looked around before he stepped out of his truck and opened the gate. He drove into the driveway and combed the area again before getting out and closing the gate back. He kept on the alert the whole time. He had enemies in Oak Cliff, but the biggest were his mother's two Rottweilers. Each of them weighed almost one hundred fifty pounds, and neither of them was too crazy about visitors. JC had been a light snack for them once or twice and wasn't in the mood for a repeat. He moved cautiously towards the front door, thinking the dogs were in the backyard and hadn't heard him come in.

He gently knocked on the door. Almost immediately, the Rotts were viciously barking, growling and bumping up against the inside of the door trying to get at him. They had startled him so severely that he ran down the porch, hopped over the guardrail, and jumped back into his truck.

He looked around for them and gradually got himself back together. He reached beneath the seat and grabbed his gun before he went back. He heard his mother yelling at the Rotts from behind the door, and then it slowly opened. A voice came from behind it, "Come on Jonathan, baby. It's ok."

He tucked the gun in his waist and pulled his shirt out to cover it. He entered slowly and saw the Rotts lying on the floor in the living room waiting to see who Momma had discarded them for. JC closed the door and slowly turned around. Neither of them had moved, but their growls were synchronized, symbolizing their shared dislike for him. JC's steps became quicker as he moved hastily from the living room to the kitchen. His mother stood at the stove stirring a pot of chicken stew with a large metal spoon.

"Hey, baby!" she said as she gave him a big hug

"Hey, Momma. Why you got them dogs in the house?"

"Because it gets hot out there, baby. I don't want 'em to have a heat stroke."

"They act like the heat's already messed 'em up."

"Stop being mean, Jonathan." she chuckled. "They just be playing with you."

"Well, I don't like the way they play."

"...What's this I hear about you robbing folks, Jonathan?"

"What'cha cooking, Momma?"

"Don't play with me boy! You want me to go up beside your

head with this spoon?"

"No..."

"Then talk to me, Darn it!"

"Momma you can't believe everything you hear. You know I promised you."

"Yeah! You promised me how many times? ...Baby, I don't want to see you laid out in them streets because you were stealing somebody's things. Now, you have businesses. Why you gotta go out and do wrong? You gotta do the right thing, baby. Don't throw your life away. Do the right thing."

"...But Momma..."

"No buts, boy! —No buts," his mother said as she slid a bowl of stew in front of him. "I've seen too much nonsense to see my boy lose his life behind greed." JC lowered his head to sample the stew and noticed that the table was new. He had grown up in this house eating at the same wobbly wooden table every day, but today he sat a fancy oak table with matching seats. As he raised his head, he noticed that the old China cabinet had been replaced, and the new one matched the table and chairs. The whole kitchen and dining room had been redone.

"Where this stuff come from? This looks like $5,000."

"It's $12,000 furniture, and mind your business."

"What? $12,000? You don't have that kind of money to spend on furniture."

"Which is why you should've bought it for me," she replied as the dogs walked through the kitchen door growling at JC. "Sit!" she yelled, and both dogs lowered their bottoms to the floor and closely monitored the rest of the conversation. "...don't think I forgot what we were talking about." JC paused and assessed the situation. On one hand he had an angry mother whose backhand rivaled Serena Williams', and on the other he had two Rotts waiting to tear him limb from limb.

"Uh...no, Momma, no...It's just that I owe somebody a lot of money, and I have to pay them back pretty quick."

"Then why don't you pay them?"

"It's not that simple, Momma. It's not the money that's an issue. It's the interest on it. You wouldn't understand." JC's mother knew her son, and this kind of worry couldn't be brought on by anyone. She sat at the table next to him and grabbed his hand.

"Who is it, baby?"

"Nobody. You don't know him."

"What!" she yelled as she slapped the spoon against the table. It sounded like a shotgun had fired and both Rotts hurried to their feet and started to growl and inch towards the table. "Sit!" she yelled to Ike and Tina, and again, they lowered their bottoms to the floor. "When I ask you something, I want an answer! You hear me?" his mother continued in a voice that was just louder than the growling dogs.

"Momma, you're upsetting the dogs."

"Boy!"

"Ok! His name is Antonio, but he's not from around here."

"Antonio, what?"

"What?"

"Antonio, what?" she yelled.

"Antonio Ruiz." JC uttered as he looked up at his mother. She sat straight up in her seat with an uneasy look on her face.

"How long have you known this Antonio?" she whispered.

"...Since I was thirteen. He helped me out of a jam one time and has been trying to get me to come work for him every since." A tear dropped from his mother's eyes, and she gripped his hand a little tighter. She then released the spoon and took hold of both of his hands.

"Jonathan," she says, "Is this why you've been taking people's things?" JC looked down at the table and never answered.

"Momma, I have to go," he said. "Thank you for the soup."

"Okay baby," she replied. "Don't you worry about that money issue, now, Momma will see what she can do to help you." He chuckled at her words and gave her a hug. When they stood up, the Rotts jumped to their feet and started barking. JC's mother yelled for them to sit and JC passed to the front door and quickly shut it behind him. The ride home was pleasant, and his day came to a close with the thought of his loving mother on his mind.

CHAPTER THREE

It was 4:00 a.m. Sunday morning and the streets were unusually calm. The trees gently swayed as their leaves rustled under the brawn of a brisk wind. The air was cool and clammy and carried the scents of flowers and freshly cut grass. The dew had begun to form, and an eerie silence prevailed, the kind that often time meant something was wrong. There wasn't a dog barking, a bird chirping, or even a streetlight buzzing. Only the sound of a lone cricket resonated from a nearby bush.

Everything seemed to be moving in slow motion: like it was being fed frame by frame through a film projector. The chirps of the cricket became increasingly rhythmic and seemed to mark the seconds of a countdown. A white flatbed pickup slowly approached with a man and woman inside. The driver pulled up to the curb and steps out onto the grass. Chirp! The woman lowered her head to light a cigarette, and the man reached into his pocket and pulled out a wad of cash. He counted the assortment of bills as he walked up to the house and rapped on the door. Knock! Knock! Knock! –Chirp! The cricket sounded. The door opened. Chirp! Chirp! There was an exchange between the driver and the man inside. Blam! The door flew wide open, and the driver ran inside followed by a platoon of men in helmets and black fatigues. "Freeze! Show me your hands!" they yelled as they stormed the house. Their guns were held high prepared to fire. They came from the front and the rear almost simultaneously. They ran through the living room, kitchen, lounge, media rooms, bathrooms, and garage in a matter of minutes. Everyone in the house had been tied up with plastic tie handcuffs and dragged into the front room.

"Where's the safe!" one of the men yelled as he waved his gun at the victims.

"What safe? There's no safe in here!" one of them replied.

Then as two of the platoon members held the victims at gunpoint and threatened them not to move, another began to load them one by one into the back of a large black truck. Their execution was quick and precise.

Another part of the team had already begun to pull the baseboards loose. They lifted the carpet, opened the backs of the televisions, radios, washing machine and dryer. The computers were taken. The walls were ripped open, and the attic was thoroughly searched.

An ambulance pulled up to the curb, and two people jumped out of the cab and ran into the house with small toolboxes in their hands. A loud sawing noise was resonating from one of the bathrooms. Eight minutes had passed, and the two men from the ambulance brought a body bag out on a stretcher. Then there was a familiar sound. Chirp! One of the platoon members then pressed a button on his radio and listened to a voice in his headset. He uttered a couple of odd words and numbers and then yelled, "Ok boss. Bring it in."

Just then a large Mack wrecker backed into the yard. All the neighbors had come to their doors and were trying to see what was happening. Another body bag was brought from the house. Two unmarked cars had blocked the road on each side with their emergency lights flashing.

The crowd grew larger as yet another body bag was brought out. The wrecker driver looked over for a split second as he donned a pair of heavy gloves and pulled a lever on the side of the truck. The thirty-five ton boom, let out, and the cable slowly began to unreel.

He fed it in through the bedroom window and into the bathroom where the sawing sound emanated. You could see the sparks flying in the bathroom from outside the windows. The wrecker driver was given a signal by one of the platoon members inside.

He then walked over to the truck and took hold of one of the levers, and with a slight movement of his hand the cable began to spool. Once the slack had been removed from the cable, a voice from inside yelled, "Let her rip!"

At his command, the wrecker driver hit the lever again. The cable jerked a couple of times and then cut down through the window frame as the cable was drawn taut. The motor from the winch whined, and the front end of the truck looked as if it was about to rise when the sound of a large explosion rung from the house as the concrete floor gave way. BOOM! The entire house rattled, and the cable began to spool at an accelerated rate.

The safe had been ripped from the bathroom floor and pulled through the bedroom window. The entire wall nearly collapses as it exited. It was about five feet tall and four feet deep. It was quickly loaded onto a flatbed truck, strapped down and draped with a large canvas tarp.

In just under 18 minutes the house had been stormed and cleared, and every car, truck, wrecker, and ambulance were gone.

Across town in the city of Arlington, a similar raid transpired just two hours earlier. That one reportedly took all of eight minutes, but there wasn't a safe involved. Altogether there were five drug raids in the Metroplex that weekend, and it would appear that a crackdown had begun.

JC woke up in his recliner just after 8:00 AM with the TV still on from the night before. He got up and walked to the kitchen to get a glass of water. While he was pouring it, a special bulletin flashed on the local station.

A University Park drug lab was raided at 4:00 a.m. this morning. Six men were arrested and at least three others were carried away by EMT. Residents of the prestigious University Park community said they had no idea that such a place existed in their neighborhood and are glad the police did something about it.

JC sat down in his recliner and watched as one of the eyewitnesses gave his account of what happened.

"It was like watching that TV show about cops. They were dressed in all black and all about business. No one even knew they were here until the ambulance showed up."

"Can you tell us a little about the gun fight?" the newscaster asked as she flipped her bangs to the side. *"I didn't hear any gunshots, just an explosion when that box came flying out the window. Like I said, no one even knew they were here until we heard the sirens from the ambulance. Some people say they woke up to a grinding noise, but I didn't hear all that."*

"Thank you, sir," she replied as she flipped the bangs on the other side and faced the camera. *"University Park Police*

*Department has not released an official statement on the raid
but has indicated that every effort is being made to reduce crime
in our neighborhoods. Also in today's news, President Reagan
announced that the United States will continue to provide
humanitarian support to the Polish through various relief
organizations..."*

JC had fallen back asleep long before the reporter had
finished her report and ten o'clock had come and gone before
his eyes opened again. "Where does the time go?" he said aloud
as he rose from his chair, stretched and let out a huge yawn.

A faint humming was heard coming from the clothes
scattered about the floor. It was his pager. It had been vibrating
repeatedly all morning. He grabbed it from his pants pocket and
stumbled over a shoe as he flipped through the numbers on his
way back to the kitchen. He stopped in front of the refrigerator,
deleted a few numbers, made a mental note to call a few others
and then opened the refrigerator and looked inside. There was
milk, water, two eggs, butter and a couple of slices of bread. He
closed the door and walked into his room and made a couple of
calls. Scratching his head through his untidy mane, he came back
to the refrigerator and looked inside but a miraculous event that
would change its contents had not occurred. "Guess it's gonna
be a Williams Chicken day," he said audibly.

Just then there was a knock at the door. KNOCK! KNOCK!
KNOCK! JC walked to the door and peered out the peephole. His
heart raced at the sight of the face on the other side of the door.
Without hesitation, he sprinted back to his pants and quickly
started to dress. He pulled up his pants, zipped the zipper and
buttoned the button. KNOCK! KNOCK! KNOCK! He reached down
and grabbed his belt, socks, shoes, and shirt and just as he stood,
the door opened. Antonio walked in and looked around. JC froze.

Antonio didn't say a word. He looked at the items scattered about the floor, the bare walls, the plaid recliner where JC previously sat, the old green vinyl couch that clashed with the dark brown carpet. He looked at JC, at his clothes, at his appearance and didn't say a word just circled him like Massa inspecting a new slave, lit a handmade Cuban cigar, puffed it a couple of times and walked out.

JC, still frozen in the center of his living room, watched Antonio and four of his men walk up the driveway to the street and get into and navy blue Cadillac Fleetwood. Who knows what this was all about? It could have been about JC knowing that Antonio knew where he lived or it could have been that Antonio was looking for something or was just flexing his muscles, showing JC and all others that nothing escaped his eyes, grew beyond his control or extended beyond his reach. Then again, he could have just been saying hello in his own special way.

After the car pulled off, JC's frozen body thawed and the clothes he had held fell to the floor. He wiped the sweat from his brow and walked to the bathroom to shower; knowing that his perspiration would easily wash away, but the lethal combination of confusion, fear and anxiety that Antonio stirred up in him had to be stripped away and never allowed to fester and form intimidation. It was time to put in some work.

CHAPTER FOUR

Just after 5:00 p.m. a blue 1979 Corvette with dual white racing stripes sped down a narrow road in Oak Cliff. It locked its brakes just as it passed a yellow and white house and skid almost sideways into the next driveway. The driveway was occupied by several drug dealers and their friends selling drugs, drinking miscellaneous poisons and shooting dice. They all scrambled to get out of the way, some of them panicking and tripping over each other in the process. Half a second after the car stopped the driver's door flew open and Treasure stepped out.

She was about 5'7 with high yellow skin and a large reddish brown Afro. She had a thin waist and upper body with thick legs and thighs. Her hazel eyes were hidden behind huge round-framed shades that swallowed half her face. Chocolate colored form-fitting suede pants and a black sleeveless zipper-front top covered her frame while a complementing set of black boots adorned her feet.

Time stopped, and everyone stared as she rapidly approached with her hair bouncing with each step. She had the overwhelming appearance of a movie star and the undeniable grit of gladiator. She was tall, sexy, and packing a pistol in both hands. JC's Suburban had pulled up behind her, and both of the front doors flew open. JC exited the driver's side with his sawed-off shotgun drawn. The audience began to scatter, and potential patrons passed without stopping. Deuce hopped out the passenger's side of the Suburban and sprinted across the lawn with a Colt Defender in his hand. He rushed past Treasure and rammed the door hard enough to jar it from its hinges. Two shots were fired at him as he fell over the dislodged door. One of them grazed his shoulder, but the other one missed. JC was right behind Deuce. He fired the shotgun at Tony, the man he gave charge of the crack house, but Tony had run from the living room, through the kitchen, and out the back door before JC got past the front room.

Tony ran around the house and backed up the driveway towards the street, but just as he passed the mailbox Treasure fired two shots that pierced him in his right hand and left thigh. The gun dropped from his hand, and he fell flatly onto his face. JC and Treasure rushed up the driveway as Tony struggled to turn over. He raised himself up onto his left elbow and grabbed his upper left thigh and clinched his right hand tightly above his chest. He cowered at the site of JC approaching and immediately began to beg for his life.

"JC. Man, I'm sorry. I didn't mean to... I mean—Hey, man. What's wrong? What I do? Don't kill me, man. They lying. I ain't do nothing. What they say? I bet they lying. Man. Don't kill me, JC..."

"The Crip Keeper says you were short twenty dollars."

"Twenty dollars? Man, I got twenty dollars in my pocket. You can take it. Man. JC. Man. Don't kill me, man. Its twenty dollars, Man. I'll give you forty dollars..."

"You think your life's worth forty dollars?"

"Yeah! Naa. Noooo. Man, I ain't nothing. I ain't even worth killing. Just give me another chance, man. Please!"

By this time Deuce had made it up the driveway. He had taken his shirt and ripped it apart to make a dressing for his shoulder. JC and Treasure looked up as he approached. Tony saw him coming and started to beg more intensely.

"JC. Man, kill me before that fool gets up here. Please! Shoot me." Treasure lifted her gun to grant his wish, but JC lifted his hand to stop her. Deuce approached yelling at the top of his lungs.

"You trying to kill me?"

"No! No..."

"Yes, you were. What's this?" Deuces said as he motioned towards his shoulder and began to kick him repeatedly. "You. Wanna. Kill. Me..." Deuce shouted while kicking Tony each time he spoke a word until JC stepped in and read Tony the Miranda Rights of Thieves.

The three of them left Tony in front of the crack house scared to move, scared to speak and scared to know what tomorrow would bring. However, when the authorities arrived in response to a neighbors 911 call, there were no gunshot victims, drug dealers, drug users, and of course, no drugs present.

Deuce had been taken to a friend of JC's to be looked at. They were there less than 10 minutes, long enough for Deuce's flesh wound to be cleaned, stitched up and bandaged.

JC advised him to lay low for a couple of weeks to allow his wound to heal. Deuce immediately protested and declared that he was more than capable of handling things, despite his injury. JC then conceded and allowed him to continue overseeing his street interests as long as Treasure accompanied him on all drops, pickups, and spot checks. Deuce had only to glance at her once before responding, "Yeah, she can ride with me, long as she knows I'm running thangs."

"Yeah, baby," Treasure replied. "You're running thangs."

"I like this broad, JC. Where you say she from?" Deuce said as he eyed her figure.

"...Let's say New Orleans" JC replied, "Now, is everything copasetic?"

"Yeah," Deuce and Treasure replied at once.

"Cool," he replied, "Treasure, take Deuce home."

"Take me to get some gin!" Deuce yelled as the last stitch was drawn taut.

That night JC drove by Xavier's on Lake June. He pulled up to the clay pot colored building with the beige, red and white striped awnings and stepped out of his truck. The valet took his keys with a courteous smile and wished him a great evening. As the valet pulled away, JC unbuttoned his top two shirt buttons and took a rare moment to take in the beauty of the eye-catching scenery. Xavier's had outside seating where patrons could relax in beautiful sandstone colored chairs that had plush seat cushions in them that matched the beige, red and white striped, table cloths and parasols. The veranda and breezeway were adorned with enough shade trees and tropical plants to give Xavier the feel of a private paradise in the middle of the city. JC smiled and proceeded to the entrance.

He stepped through the front door and walked through the main dining room. The restaurant was nearly full. The air was filled with the aroma of assorted wines, savory steaks, and sweet-smelling accompaniments. The light sounds of conversations and tableware were emanating from every direction. A live band played soft jazz on an elevated off-centered stage. The high ceilings were bejeweled with glistening chandeliers and carried the band's soft melodies effortlessly. The waiters and waitresses were all smiling. Everyone was doing their part in making this and every night at Xavier's a night to remember.

When JC entered the kitchen, there were busboys tending to the tableware, waiters, and waitresses committed to the customer's orders and cooks dedicated to the assembly of masterpieces. Amid all these happenings his eyes fell on Xavier, a man he had known all of his life. Xavier was his next-door neighbor in his youth, and their mothers were good friends. He was like a brother to JC, and it was rare that they were ever apart. There have never been two people so much alike and yet, so very different. JC's mother used to say they were like oil and water: never mixing but slippery as hell when together.

Xavier was tall and slightly heavy, built like a football player and a half. He was extremely quick on his feet, good with his hands and black as volcanic rock. The kids used to joke that his eyes were the only thing that kept him from disappearing when night fell. Some called him the shadow. Some called him Smoke or Darth Vader, but nearly all of them wished he wasn't so strong because every now and then Xavier would grab one of them by the neck and it would take five or six others to wrestle him down and free his victim. Other times he was gentle, forgiving and trying to find the good in every situation. His lifelong dream was to be a chef like his late father and thanks to JC's baleful role in society; he had the opportunity to fulfill that dream. He looked up from the lobsters he was preparing and noticed JC. He smiled, finished instructing his assistants and walked over to his lifelong buddy.

"What's up boss?" Xavier said.

"The Crypt Keeper says you're short."

"She better count it up again!" They chuckled amongst themselves and exchanged hand gestures as they shook each other's hand.

"So how are we tonight?" JC said as he looked over the Lobsters.

"We cool ...probably gone have another $6,000 day. A few more of these and I can buy you out."

"How you know I wanna sell?"

"You gone have to sell."

"What?"

"You're eventually gonna have to sell. You have your hands in too many fires, JC."

"Yeah, been thinking 'bout that, but I need to make this money while I can."

"That's cool, but make the money and don't let the money make you."

"Where you get that stupidness from?"

"...Yo momma." They laughed again.

"You know your mom's an ancient proverb preaching, magic knee scrape medicine making..."

"Boy, don't talk 'bout my momma."

"Boy? Okay. I'll talk 'bout your daddy then. Wait! Who's ya, daddy?" A couple of chuckles followed that comment, but no answer was spoken. JC gave his friend a hug and began to walk away when Xavier yelled back to JC, "Hey, did the Keeper really say I was short?"

"Nah," JC replied, as he looked back, "The Reaper feeds the Keeper, not the other way around. You don't ever have to worry 'bout the keeper." "Thanks, man. I appreciate that."

"Don't mention it."

He walked from the kitchen to the stage and sat on the bench next to the piano player. The band had a brief intermission and was just returning to their positions. The piano player asked JC if there was something he would like to hear. JC smiled as he looked down at the keys, and replied, "Yeah, when I was young my mother used to play the piano. That was before her arthritis started acting up on her." he chuckled, "She would always play that "Amazing Grace" song." The piano player then began to softly play the song JC had heard his mother play a hundred times before. After the first couple of stanzas, the band instinctively joined in. A few customers paused and glanced up at the band, but most of them carried on as they had been before. JC chuckled a time or two and nodded to the piano player, who gave "Amazing Grace" a light jazz groove.

A quarter-way through the song JC noticed a woman in the audience standing up from her table. Her face could not be seen from his position, but something about her manner captured his attention. He watched her step away. Her long legs, defined thighs, small waistline, perky chest and toned arms were all in concert, but her facial view was still impaired by her long curly hair. However, when she looked up and pulled it away, the familiar visage warmed his heart and he immediately rose from his seat. A large boyish smile came over his face as he gawked at her beauty and basked in her glamour. It was Tina, but unlike the moments of their first meeting; on this occasion, she would command his attention.

He hurried down the narrow steps opposite the stage and along the wall towards the foyer. One of the waiters slowed him with a request from Xavier. JC nodded and patted the waiter on the shoulder while still glancing across the room at Tina. "Tell him I'll be there in a moment," he said and continued to the foyer.

Tina hadn't noticed JC because she was not alone. However, she wasn't with the two friends he had met before, but someone altogether different. She had reserved this pivotal moment for her high school sweetheart, Ronald Thurgood, a young man whose evening was obviously not going according to plan. Ronald gazed upon Tina with a stern Momma's look on his face and spoke through his gritted teeth.

"I can't believe you're breaking up with me."

"It has been over between us, Ronald. Why are you making this so hard?"

"I've been good to you!" he replied, as he grabbed her hand. Tina snatched away from him sharply and stopped midway up the breezeway.

"Yes, Ronald," she replied, "you were good to me, La'Shunda and half the girls at the school."

"What are you saying?"

"I'm saying the same thing I've been saying all night, Ronald. This is it: our last dance. When we depart tonight, we depart forever."

"I was good to you, girl!"

"...Enjoy the rest of your evening, Ronald."

"Hey! Don't walk away from me," Ronald yelled, as he violently snatched her arm and pulled her toward him.

"Hey!" JC uttered, as he approached the two of them. "How's everything going tonight?"

"It's going quite well sir," Tina replied, as she stepped back and flipped her bang to the side. I put our dinner on your tab as you kindly suggested. I hope that was ok."

"Of course," JC replied in a somewhat puzzled manner and turned to Ronald and reached out to shake his hand. Ronald denied him a handshake. He just looked over at Tina and gave her a long-lasting stare-down before peacefully walking away.

"I see you've had an interesting evening, Ms. Tina."

"...so you remember my name?"

"Yes. Tina, the friend of Sheila and Daphne, lover of cocoa, hater of coffee for no apparent reason other than that it's not cocoa."

"Very good," Tina said with a smile.

"Hey, I know you've had an eventful evening and are in a hurry to get wherever it is you're going, but if you can spare a moment, I would like to show you something."

"Show me what?"

"...Something special. Come on."

"Alright. A moment."

JC walked Tina into the back of the restaurant. The band was playing a soft jazz piece. Tina stopped just before the kitchen door and looked up at the stage.

"I love this music," she said, "I know its jazz, but it's somehow different from any other jazz I've heard."

"It's Latin Jazz: a combination of African and Latin American rhythms and jazz harmonies."

"Really?" Tina replied.

"Yeah, and these guys throw all of it together. Jazz, Boogaloo, Salsa, Ragga, Reggae, Meringue, Bossa Nova and others to produce a sound so unique that you can only experience it here at Xavier's."

"You sound like a commercial," Tina laughed.

"I just love the atmosphere. It's like a world outside of my own."

"Yeah, I heard of this place," Tina replied, "but I've never had the time or money to come by. Unlike you, you're probably here all the time."

"As a matter of fact, I am. My best friend is the chef."

"Really?"

"Yeah, I'll introduce you."

As they entered the kitchen, Tina was overwhelmed with the amount of activity. JC lead her to the grill where Xavier was turning over some steaks.

"Oh, more helpers," Xavier said when he looked over at them.

"What?" Tina cried out.

"Let me help you out," said Xavier, as he stepped over to a small room where the staff took their breaks and came out with hairnets and two aprons.

"I'm not about to work in this kitchen!" Tina uttered, "If you want me to pay for that dinner I will."

"Relax. I'm just gonna help Xavier get caught up. If you like you can have a seat in the corner over there, and I'll get to your surprise in a moment," JC said, as he grabbed an apron and began to put it on.

"...A moment?" Tina said. "You mean another moment. First, you want to show me something, now you wanna surprise me with something, like handing me a net and an apron isn't surprise enough."

"Well, I apologize, Ms. Tina, but I need to help out my friend. If there is somewhere you need to be, I understand."

JC then winked at her and walked over to the grill. Tina stood there for a moment with her arms crossed. JC worked the grill as if he was a regular at it. Each steak was prepared to Xavier's exacting standards. JC glanced over to the corner where he thought Tina would've been seated, but she wasn't there. He had prepared a few more steak orders and a few chicken breasts before Tina came around the corner with her apron and hair net on. She was covered with flour. Even in her apron she was beautiful. JC stared at her with a surprised smile on his face. Just then Xavier popped him behind the head.

"Pay attention to them steaks."

"I was," JC replied.

"...On the grill!" They both laughed. "I had a talk with your lil lady," Xavier whispered, "She's cool."

"Thanks, man."

"Don't mention it."

The kitchen closed at ten o'clock. The bus persons and wait staff were cleaning everything and preparing for the next day's business. Tina had a seat in the corner at a small table that had two bar stools on each side. JC then came up and sat at the table with her.

"So how was it?" he asked.

"It was great!" Tina replied, "I have never had so much fun in a kitchen. There are so many things that go on back here, and Xavier makes every little step from powdering pans to the order you add ingredients seem so important. I felt like I was part of something tonight. –Something enormous."

"Enormous?"

"Yes, huge."

"I know what the word means. I just never looked at it like that."

"You should broaden your horizons."

"Yeah, like you did tonight?"

"Yes," Tina Laughed.

"Excuse me, people," Xavier said as he walked up pushing a

cart with several dishes on top of it. "I believe this is the part of the evening that you've been waiting for."

Tina sat up in her seat anxious to see what he had. JC took notice of her demeanor: so simple, so carefree and so full of life. He could see in her all the things he desired in his own life.

She pulled off the hair net, combed her hair with her fingers and leaned forward with her hands in her lap watching Xavier. He sliced a pineapple lengthwise through the crown and began to cut out the core and surrounding flesh. He placed the pineapple chunks in a chafing dish that already had sugar, pineapple, banana, orange sections and Bacardi 151 in it. It smelled like one luscious fruit instead of five individual ingredients. It was altogether spicy, sweet and pungent. He stirred the mixture together and placed it on a small flame. He then laid two plates on the table and opened another container and began to artistically arrange the fruit on the plates in two disparate half circles. The colors were astonishing: Red and yellow papaya, radiant green kiwi and deep red strawberries. He then cut the pineapple shell so that it laid flat on the plate between the fruit circle and spooned in three medium scoops of ice cream. The sugar, pineapple, orange and banana mixture were then lit with a large match. Tina jumped from her seat.

"Xavier!"

"Relax Ms. Tina. It's a flambé," he said.

Everyone laughed, and Tina returned to her seat. Once the flame died, Xavier poured the fruit and their sauce over the ice cream. Tina closed her eyes and deeply inhaled the aroma. When her eyes opened again, JC and Xavier were attentive to her reaction. She glowed all over like a five year old looking over their birthday cake.

"This is wonderful, guys, absolutely wonderful," she said.

"This is my Tropical Jubilee. It's JC's favorite," boasted Xavier. "You guys have fun and enjoy your dessert."

Xavier smiled at the two of them and walked away pushing his cart. It was obvious that Tina was impressed.

After Xavier's Tropical Jubilee, an hour of talking and eating the remaining fruit from each other's plates, JC and Tina were carrying on like old friends. Tina left his side only once to freshen up. When she returned, her hair, dress and accessories were as they were when she first arrived. One would have never known that this was a woman who had just spent an hour working in the kitchen. However, time had passed quickly, and he could see that it was approaching the time when she would have to leave. He dreaded this moment, as did she, but their warm conversation continued on as they walked out to the parking lot.

He offered to walk her to her car, but she told him it wasn't necessary. He, nonetheless, insisted on being a gentleman and naturally walked her to the driver's side of the car. A nervous look came over her face as he looked over at her and reached for the door handle. She looked down at the door and then back up at him without saying a word. He then leaned against the car and gazed deep into her eyes.

"You're a beautiful woman, Ms. Tina," he said.

"Thanks," Tina replied as she looked back down at the door.

"When can I see you again?"

"Um, I don't think I should start seeing someone so soon. I mean, I just broke up with Ronald two hours ago."

JC stood up, still holding onto the door handle with his right hand.

"I know," he said, "That's so unfortunate. Ol' boy must be crushed."

"I doubt it," Tina replied. "It's been two hours. He's likely with

La'Shunda Williams by now."

"Who is that?"

"Some cheerleader type. All ass and no brains."

They both laughed at that remark, and Tina gave him the lowdown on all of Ronald's escapades. She said her and La'Shunda were mortal enemies like King Kong and Godzilla for a hundred different reasons.

"So whatcha gonna do kick her butt or what?" he asked.

"No. I'm just gonna pray for her."

"Pray for her? You sound like my momma. Pray for her. You better handle your business and prey on her."

"I'm gonna pray for you too...talking 'bout preying on somebody. Is that what you do?"

"I do what I gotta."

"What you gotta?"

"That's right, what I gotta." More laughing surrounds their conversation then Tina becomes more serious.

"When we met there was a guy putting bags in your car. Was that drugs?"

"No."

"Don't lie!"

"It wasn't drugs. It was money to buy drugs," JC said, with a small snicker.

"You seem like a nice guy Jonathan, but I'm about to go to college. Start my life; be somebody. I don't want to be involved with any drug dealers."

"What 'bout bank robbers?" JC said, and they both laughed. She then handed him her phone number.

"Call me. Maybe we can do something next weekend."

"Ok," he replied, as he pushed the button and pulled on the door handle. However, the door didn't open. "I can see that it's unlocked," JC said while still tugging on it. Tina placed her left hand on her forehead and closed her eyes embarrassed at the situation.

"It's ok, Jonathan. I'll just get in on the other side."

"No, I can get it open," he replied.

Within minutes, JC, Xavier, and two other men were at the car taking their turn at tugging at the door handle. Tina was too embarrassed to tell them that the door had been jammed shut for over a year. Then suddenly there was a popping noise. Pank! One of the men had pulled the door handle off. Tina lowered herself to the pavement and buried her face in her hands. JC quickly stepped over to assist her.

"...You a'ight, Ms. Tina?" He said as he kneeled down beside her. "Don't worry 'bout the door. I'll have my mechanic fix it tomorrow."

One of the guys had entered the car from the passenger's side and tried to open the door but couldn't. He then attempted to climb back out the same way he got in, but his foot got caught on a loose wire causing him to trip. All the men laughed as he stood up and pulled the wires from around his ankle. There was speaker wire on one end and electrical wires on the other. "It may still start," one of the men joked as the horn sounded in one continuous blast.

"I think I'm going to be sick," Tina murmured.

"-You want me to give you a ride?" JC asked.

"Yes. Yes, please," Tina replied.

"Ok let me get my truck. I'll be right back." "

Ok," Tina said, as she looked over at the car ashamed that she hadn't left when she previously thought to and embarrassed that her greatest date ever would end with this ashamed moment. However, he returned in no time. Hurrying to her side, he assisted her to her feet and Xavier, who had disconnected the car battery and ceased the never-ending blare of the horn, handed over her keys.

"Good night, Tina," Xavier said kindly as JC helped her into the truck.

"Good night," she said softly as she took one last gaze at her Impala and then looked down shamefully at her lap as if she had lost an old friend or betrayed a first love. She twiddled her fingers nervously as she and JC pulled away. They were nearly silent as they rode up Lake June to Cooper Road and then down to Harwood, but JC eased the awkwardness of the moment with light music and engaging conversation. She didn't respond much at first, but eventually loosened up and began to speak to him as she had before. He chuckled at the change in her demeanor and watched her more than he did the road. Tina began to tell him about her accomplishments in high school, her aspirations for the future and her bouts with knucklehead men. They laughed together from time to time, and Tina made no mention of the fact that she knew that he was purposely taking the scenic route to her house.

In the course of their conversation, she confessed that she didn't want him to walk her to the car because she was ashamed of it and by no means wanted to be seen climbing in from the passenger's side. JC was touched by her honesty. He smiled and chuckled several times during her confession and on one occasion laughed so hard that he drove onto the curb startling the both of them. Tina took that opportunity to tell him the truth about the car. She told him that she had driven the car into a ditch the year before, and the door had been stuck ever since. He glanced over at her and smiled and then looked back down the road. Tina's confidence suddenly dissipated and she looked back down at her lap, ashamed all over again, twiddling her fingers and searching for words. Then after a brief moment, she suggested that they turn around and go back and get the car. JC considered it for only a second before he grabbed her hand and said, "Don't worry 'bout it, Ms. Tina. My friend can fix it for almost nothing." She simply smiled and looked back down at her lap. It was comical to him that she had become so easily embarrassed by the events surrounding her car. However, he understood that this was a much different experience for a woman than it would've been for a man. Likewise, if there was anyone in the world who deserved to have a decent and dependable vehicle, it was Ms. Tina. It was obvious that he was glad that their night had been unexpectedly extended, and though Tina's manner was unassuming, he knew that she liked him just the same.

When they arrived at Tina's house, he assisted her out the truck and courteously walked her to the door. The house was only a couple of yards from the driveway, but they walked together leisurely and cherished the last few moments of the evening. JC was earnestly trying to maintain a gentleman's posture, and Tina was sincerely trying to maintain a lady's modesty, but each of them, despite their efforts, showed fleeting moments of compromise. They walked closely brushing each other continually: Each of them flirting with the other and hinting at a desire for more. Something was happening between them: something unique, intense and beautiful.

Her smile was in full bloom as they stepped upon the porch. She stopped and reached into her purse for her keys, and he stood aside and watched her. His eyes rolled down his nose and into her bosom, from her bosom to the flatness of her stomach and then further. She smiled at him as she withdrew the keys and unlocked the door, but just as she was stepping inside, she stopped again and looked back at him.

"Thank you for a wonderful evening," she said. "If I hadn't stayed at the restaurant tonight I would have been here all night crying."

"You're welcome, Ms. Tina," JC replied.

"...And stop calling me that. ...You make me sound old."

"Ok then, -and you can call me JC."

"No. That's disrespecting ya momma."

"What you mean?"

"Your momma named you Jonathan, not JC."

"Whatever."

"Whatever?" Tina chuckled.

"Yeah," JC said as he pulled her close, "whatever you want to call me is ok with me as long as you are sure to call me." A small kiss was shared between them, and Tina looked deep into his eyes, paused for a moment and then replied.

"I'll call you as long as you do right."

"...Do right by you?" Asked JC.

"Do right period."

"In that case, it was nice knowing ya."

"What!" Tina exclaimed.

"I'm just joking," his chuckle reduced to a subtle smile.

"I'll see what I can do."

"Ok. Jonathan."

"See ya later, Ms. Tina. Oh! Do you have a ride to work tomorrow?"

"Yeah, I can have one of my girls take me."

"A'ight then. See ya later."

"Bye!"

He walked back to his truck looking up at the sky. The night was clear, the moon was full, and the stars were bright. As he opened his door, he looked around at the beautifully manicured yard, the large Oak trees and the vastness of the sky. Tina watched him from the window and then looked at the sky as he did. He gently shut the door and walked to the back of his truck and sat on the bumper. Several minutes later, Tina stepped outside with her arms crossed over her chest and hands resting on each shoulder. She fixed her eyes on JC. He had the look of a weary soldier, one who had fought so long he had forgotten his cause and yielded his will to carry on. She stepped down the small set of steps that precede the porch and eased her way to his side. She placed her hand on his shoulder and sat next to him on the bumper.

"Are you ok?" She asked.

"Yeah," he replied softly.

"Then, why are you still here?"

"...I just realized that I've never taken the time to appreciate the beautiful things. I spend all of my time looking at the ugly side of things...and the simple things. The meaningful and beautiful things have always escaped me and the past couple of hours with you have shown me that. I envy the way you blush at the smell of pineapples and the way you respond to the sounds of soft music. The life in you exposes what's dead in me. ...You're genuine, nothing like the people I'm used to. You're probably the only honestly good person I know."

"Is this some kinda line?" Tina asks as she flips her hair to the side.

"No. It's what I'm feeling," JC replied. "Look up there at all those shining stars and the moon reflecting the rays of the sun. Look at how they illuminate the skies above us. I was a dark empty sky with no stars, no moon, and no light until now. You're like a shooting star streaking through my life captivating me with colors and textures I've never seen, and warmth I've never felt."

"JC, you're not getting any ass tonight," Tina says, with a chuckle.

"No! Girl, please!" He resumes, "You're messing up my vibe, now. Let me do this."

"Ok, baby, go ahead."

"...Like I was saying before bighead here interrupted me..."

"Big head?"

"Yeah..."

"I know you ain't talking!"

They both laughed and continued their conversations long into the morning. The birds began to sing as the sun rose and they were still wide awake, caught up in each other and falling quickly and intensely in love. JC reached over and gave her one last kiss before he departed --this one was long, deep and passionate. Tina caught herself and slowly pulled away. JC then cupped her hands in his and whispered, "Don't worry Ms. Tina, I won't let you down." Tina didn't reply to his comment. She just gazed into his eyes and softly said goodnight, although it was morning, before scurrying back into the house. JC, likewise, moseyed down the steps and back to his truck. Tina watched him from behind her curtain as he backed out of the driveway and drove off.

She wiped her brow as she left the window and tied up her hair. Her mother was still fast asleep when she entered her room and gently kissed her on the forehead. Mrs. Sanchez had a merry smile on her face and seemed to be dreaming. Tina sat on the edge of the bed and looked down at her. Her age showed on her face and suggested that she had become a well of wisdom. She was so strong, and yet, so very frail. A single tear rolled down

Tina's cheek as she pulled the covers up on her mother. Tina wiped the tear as she stood and wandered back to the hall that led to her room. She was maybe halfway when she stopped and leaned against the wall. Sadness had donned her face as her head filled with thoughts, and she slowly sank back into her reality. She turned and faced the opposing wall, wiping her face with both hands. Just then her eyes focused on the lower portion of the wall and the countless number of Crayon markings, blue and green, scribbled upon the eggshell-colored paint. The patterns were such that only a two-year-old could make out. Tina smiled, perhaps remembering scribbling on the wall or her mother's reaction to her doing it. Just above the markings were the many pictures of their life's past: her terrible twos, treacherous threes and so on. It seemed like her mother had lined hundreds of pictures along that wall in nearly perfect order, but her eyes settled on a lone picture of her as a small child being held by her mother. She stood up and touched the glass and her tears, again, began to fall.

Tina, no doubt, wondered about her father. Her mother had told her so much about him. He was a fine husband to her mother and an overall good man. However, he seemed to have taken a part of Mrs. Sanchez with him when he died because she was never quite the same afterwards. She once told Tina that she wanted to hang around long enough to see her graduate and then she would be off to see her husband and the Lord. Every since then, Tina had been afraid of losing her mother. She had reached a point where she could not be completely happy with the positive things that had happened for the fear of the negative things that could happen. She was stuck, holding firm to the picture of her family's past, in the passageway between where she had been and where she was headed.

CHAPTER FIVE

The next afternoon JC called Mike's Garage on Cooper Road and asked Mike to look at Tina's car. Meanwhile, he ran some errands. One of his stops was to S&P, a mom and pops store off Ledbetter. He pulled up to the store with his windows down. The north wind provided a nice breeze. He got out of the Suburban and spoke with a few of the neighborhood drug dealers. They all knew him, recognized his truck and were sure to speak or at least nod their head in recognition upon seeing him. One of them stepped around the corner of the building when he saw JC pull up. JC noticed him but gave it little attention. It was Deuce's Job to chase down JC's money. Besides, many of these guys had already heard about Tony and were sure to handle their relationship with JC with care. After all, Tony wasn't the first and wouldn't be the last. He was just the most recent. None of these street dealers worked for JC but were indirectly supplied by him through his crack houses. Sometimes, when their purchases were large enough, they were given a meager discount so that they could turn a slightly larger profit for themselves.

As JC approached the entrance and reached for the door, a man in a wheelchair rolled up behind him. His given name was Oscar English, but everyone called him Gimme. He was almost dark as Xavier and looked like he may have once been pretty athletic. His shoulders were broad, and his arms were thick and muscular. The rumor was that he was paralyzed from a car accident some years back. Only a handful of people knew why JC was so kind to him. Most people just ignored him and strolled by him like he didn't exist, as if he wasn't even there.

When JC saw Gimme approaching, he stopped and held the door open for him to roll in.

"Hey JC, can a brotha get a dollar for sump'n to eat?" Gimme yelled.

"You hungry?"

"Hell yeah! You hungry?"

"...as hell," JC replied, as they both laughed as if something was amusing about hunger. Then Gimme's bloodshot eyes focused intently on JC.

"Eighteen minutes was too long, man."

"Yeah. ...complications with the package."

"Yeah, but eighteen minutes, man?"

"Mario's information wasn't entirely reliable," JC continued. "That box was held down by two eight-inch beams and then cemented in before the foundation was laid."

"Who does that?"

"Nobody does that. I've been thinking 'bout that. The police were there five minutes after we left. I think we were set up."

"What do you mean?"

"Ride with me."

"Cool!"

"Where we going?"

"To see the Keeper."

"Hell No! Man, I'll catch you when you get back."

"What the hell you scared of? Roll around the block and wait for me in the alley."

"Why?"

"Cause I'm not carrying your heavy ass." They both laughed, and Gimme started rolling away.

"...Don't forget to get me one of them poke-chop sandwiches," Gimme yelled back to JC.

"Yeah! Gimme ya money!" JC replied. They each laughed more as Gimme rolled out the door and around the corner as he was instructed. JC bought two pork chop sandwiches, two bags of chips and two bottles of water. The cashier placed everything in a large plastic bag and JC gave him a $10 bill and told him to keep the change. He pushed the metal-barred door open and headed back to his Suburban. As he was getting in, a guy walked to his truck with a spray bottle and a couple of sheets of newspaper.

"Man, let me clean your windows for a couple of dollars."

"Whatcha gon' buy?" JC replied.

"What?"

"What you gon' buy? Drugs? Food? If I give you a couple of dollars, you're gonna go out and buy some drugs. Right?" JC got out the suburban with a pistol in his hand and walked towards the man and put it to his head. "Why don't you just ask me for some drugs? ...They selling for me anyway. Curtis!" JC yelled at one of the men standing in front of the store. "This man wants some drugs. He wants to die." JC then pressed the pistol hard against the man's head. "You still want a couple of dollars for some drugs?"

"No! I wanted to get me something to eat," the man replied

as he lowered himself to the ground and curled into the fetal position.

JC looked at him closely and attentively. People had gathered around watching. JC went back to his Suburban and grabbed the bag of food and sat it at the man's feet and looked up at the crowd.

"Nobody sell to him. Nobody! I don't care if he shows up with a thousand dollars. You sell him a crumb, and I'll have your ass." The crowd began to disperse, and JC got back into his Suburban and drove off.

When JC pulled into the alley, Gimme got up from his wheelchair, folded it and placed it in the back of JC's Suburban.

"Where's the food, man?" Gimme asked as he got in.

"I gave it away."

"What? Your food or mine?"

"Our food. Gerald came up begging for money again."

"Man."

"Yeah, your cousin or not, next time I'ma smoke him myself."

"No, you're not."

"What?" JC yelled.

"Xavier's the closest thing you have to a brother, and you know his momma would lose it if you hurt her lil nephew."

"Forget you."

"Don't be mad at me. If you cared, you'd put him in rehab."

"Man, forget you! ...And shut the hell up with that craziness. You put him in rehab. It's your cousin."

"Forget that fool."

"Forget you."

"A'ight man, Forget me."

JC stopped at a gas station to make a call. Afterwards, they drove to Pleasant Grove and pulled into the driveway of a yellow and white wood-framed house. There was a large gravel driveway that went around the left side of the house and stopped just before the back door. JC drove around back. Gimme got out first and walked to the back of the Suburban to get his wheelchair. He sat down, put on his gloves and followed JC to the front of the house. Gimme rolled up the ramp and into the house where Scratch sat watching TV. Scratch, the pseudo name of Satan, was Sandy's nickname and the only name people knew. Her age was unknown, but everyone figured that she was around sixty. She was a large woman who had been confined to a wheelchair for most of her life. She was mean as a bag of scorpions, and her cringed face, scratchy voice, and snub-nosed .38 kept the neighbors and all others away. JC used to be her paperboy. He was the only person permitted beyond the chain-linked gate. She schooled him on the art of making money: taught him every scam, every gambler's game, and every hustler's hustle. He met her about the time he met Antonio. From the two of them, he quickly caught on to the role and rewards of the lawless and exceeded each of their expectations. Scratch was old school in every sense of the word and trusted no one, except JC. She was often referred to as the Crypt Keeper or simply the Keeper by JC's crew. She was undoubtedly the most important link in his organization. She handled the bookkeeping, hid and protected the money and controlled the assets.

JC sat on the couch on the far side of the room and gleamed into the TV. Not a word was spoken. No hi's, hellos or gestures of acknowledgment. Everyone sat watching the game show. Gimme looked at Scratch's heavily wrinkled face with disgust and peeped through the side of her bifocals. She turned and looked at him, and he looked back at the TV. Fifteen minutes passed, and JC's pager went off. He grabbed the phone and dialed the number that came up in his pager and sat it down on the table.

"Somebody page?"

"Yeah, JC?"

"Yeah! Who dis?"

"This is Mike."

"Oh! OK, what you find out? Can you fix it?"

"Yeah, but a door handle is the least of your worries. Where did you get this car?"

"It belongs to a friend."

"Man this car has a twisted frame, which is why the door is jammed. There's a serious mess under the hood, wires all over the place, oil leaks everywhere, transmission slippage. I think your friend should just junk this car and get another."

"How much to fix it all?"

"All what? This is a major job, JC. It's almost a restoration job."

"How much for a full restoration?"

"Well, you're wasting your money if you ask me, but I'll say 'bout $7,500."

"Can it be done in a week?"

"Hell no! I'll need 'bout a month."

"Have it done in a week and I'll give you $10,000."

"JC?" Click.

He hung up the phone as Treasure drove into the driveway. She had Sync with her. Sync was and Systems Security Engineer by trade, a privileged brat by birth and a thief by choice. He was nearly thirty years old. He had bushy blond hair, big ears, and an unusually pale complexion. There was nothing astonishing about his appearance at all. He was about 5'10 and slender built. He was JC's planning coordinator. Treasure was his enforcer. Scratch was his accountant, and Gimme was his eyes and ears on the street. Together they were the inner circle of a twelve-man crew that they jokingly called The Reaper.

When Sync and Treasure entered the house, JC walked into the back room, and everyone followed. There were two tables in the center of the room with six stacks of money on each. He looked over at scratch and then back at the tables.

"How much?"

"$764,987 total. $63,748 each," Scratch replied.

"Bag $200,000 and divide it again."

"That's $564,987 total. $47,082 a piece."

"Good. Put that on the books, move the money to the crypt and set payout for tomorrow evening."

"Okay ...and your cut?"

"Send $10,000 to Mike's Garage and deposit the rest.

"Ok," Scratch said. "Why so soon?"

"I was visited by Antonio this morning. His men came in like they were looking for something."

"What are you thinking?" asked Scratch.

"He knows too much 'bout our recent activity."

"You think someone's tipping him off?" Gimme asked.

"How did Mario get the reconnaissance on that job?" JC asked.

"He said he overheard a contact mention it and then cased the activity for the past month," Gimme added.

"...And then we cased it for two weeks," JC said. "The only activity we saw was a van coming and going every couple of days: Never a car, a dope-fiend, or anything out of the ordinary."

"So how'd you know this place was hot, again?" Sync asked.

"Well, one day Deuce and I followed the van and noticed that it was Victor. He pulled over at William's Chicken and parked next to another van that was the same make, model, and color.

He got out and walked inside with a backpack thrown over his shoulder. There was another guy in line in front of him with a pack thrown over his shoulder the same way, but we couldn't get close enough to see who it was. At this point, we knew we were going to hit that van when he left, but he and this guy sat down and ate.

"The problem occurred when Victor came out and got into the other van and drove off. We had to take a gamble on which van to follow."

"Damn," Sync replied. "

...So we stuck with Victor. We followed and ambushed him," JC continued. "...Donned some hoods and jacked him at the intersection of Mockingbird and Skillman. We hit him hard, clean and fast. He had no idea of who we were." JC leaned up against the table and looked at the four of them. "We kicked him out in the middle of the road. The van was carrying meat. Lots of meat, frozen and wrapped up like it had just come from the butchery. We grabbed the backpack which had $35,000 in it, but we left the meat there, all except for one pack that Deuce insisted on having. We tried to hurry back and find the other truck but couldn't locate it, so we hit his crack house. It only had 'bout $3000 in it, so we went back to Deuce's place and hung out for a minute until everything cooled down. –I started thinking, what would Victor be doing in University Park and why would he be riding around with $35,000 and a truckload of meat. It didn't make sense. That crack house doesn't put out that kind of money. He had to have sold that guy in William's Chicken something he got from the house in University Park. Something small but worth lots of money, so I started thinking it must be heroin. Victor was then off the radar a couple of days and, 'bout time we found out where he had gone, Antonio had him.

"Wardo and his crew had beaten him up pretty bad and tied him up in Antonio's dining room at Pelican Bay."

"How you know this?" Scratch asked.

"We saw him when we went to meet with Antonio Friday. Antonio knew we hit the truck but was under the impression that Victor had $100-150 thousand dollars on him."

"So Victor was planning on buying heroin with Antonio's money and skipping town or what?" Sync implied.

"No. I don't think so," JC replied, "You can't hide from Antonio. Victor knows this. I think he was going to try and turn a quick profit before Antonio missed the money, but Antonio was watching him like he's watching us.

"Victor took Antonio's money, bought heroin and resold it to that guy in William's Chicken. This has gotta be where the $35,000 came from."

"...So what would be the purpose of switching trucks," Scratch asked.

"I don't know, but it gave me enough reason to figure that that house we had staked out over there was somebody's piggybank.

"If your faces were covered when you hit Victor's truck," Treasure said, "How'd Antonio know it was you?"

"I don't know," JC replied, "but I'm curious 'bout something. If Mario cased that place for a month, why didn't he know it was Victor driving the van? The two of them are friends aren't they? He knew we would eventually hit that van."

"I saw Victor and Mario at the liquor store last week, but I didn't think nothing of it at the time, but what if Mario and Victor are working together?"

"Then Antonio would be after Mario as well," JC responded.

"Sounds like Mario switched trucks to ensure that you hit the truck that was Antonio's so that Antonio would come after you," Treasure added.

"So how come he was so chummy with me?" JC Replied. "Something's crazy 'bout this whole thing. ...Scratch, I need the money moved today. Immediately. And get with Jimmy and have all the paperwork fixed. Don't let anyone in on what we know."

"...And this Deuce," Scratch said. "Are you grooming him for a job we should know 'bout."

"No," JC replied, "He's careless. He's most effective where he is. How is he anyway?"

"Bullheaded as ever," Treasure replied. "But recovering just fine."

"Good. Get him right," he said. "We won't have time to babysit going further."

"What do you want me to do?" Treasure asked. "

Wake him up," JC replied.

CHAPTER SIX

That same day, Tina woke up to the smell of bacon, eggs, and homemade tortillas. She moseyed into the kitchen, poured a glass of orange juice and sat at the table with her mother who was enjoying her morning dose of coffee.

"Ruff night?" her mother asked as she took a seat beside her.

"No," Tina chuckled. "It was a wonderful night."

"How so?"

"I met this guy. Well...I've met him before, but somehow last night was just..."

"Yeah, just what?"

"Wonderful." Tina sighed as she began to fix herself a breakfast burrito.

"Are you having sex, girl?" her mother said sternly as she sat up in her chair.

"No, Momma!" Tina laughed. "I'm saving that for the one."

"The one? ...And which one is that?"

"Momma!" Tina laughed more dearly, "The one I marry."

"Okay! Don't be trying to be slick 'lil girl. I used to be a teenager too. I can smell a rat a mile away. Don't you go being like these 'lil girls walking up Lake June trying to find them a drug dealer or a ball player to take care of you. You take care of yourself. Then if a young man comes along with a good job and knows how to treat you, you give him a chance. Then If he manages to keep a good job and treat you right, let him call you his woman, but when you meet the one who loves his good paying job and worships the ground you walk on, that one is the one you marry."

"What if he's just cute and treats me right?"

"Hell! I've seen cute dogs that'll do what you tell 'em. Does he have a good job?"

Tina just laughed at her mother. She was very protective of her little girl, and they often shared these morning talks: these mini-sermons on life that Tina so greatly cherished but gradually lost with each passing day. Tina loved the magnificent moments of laughter, growth, bonding and reflection they had. Nonetheless, she was troubled and torn by those that reminded her of her mother's deep sorrows and ever-eroding memories. The past year had shown Tina that her mother was indeed a fighter, but her Alzheimer's was progressing rapidly for seemingly undetermined reasons, but that morning was a distinct moment of clarity and with that, Tina was pleased.

She kissed her mother on the forehead as she left for the bus, wishing she had not lied to JC about having a ride to work. None of her friends had cars, which is why Sheila and Daphne always rode with her. So on this day, they would seek their own means of transportation and for each of them that meant Dallas Area Rapid Transit.

Tina spent the greater part of the day at work making collection calls. She had just moved from part time to full time a couple of weeks prior, following her high school graduation, and was still adjusting to her new schedule. At 9:00 PM she grabbed her bag and rose from her cubicle appearing to be dreading the idea of catching the bus home. Everyone was saying "goodbye", "see ya tomorrow" and "have a nice night." She managed a smile and waved at a few of them as she headed for the elevator. Again and again, Tina glanced at her watch, monitoring the time. She had about eight minutes to get ten minutes away. The elevator seemed unusually slow as if it was being held on one of the lower floors. When it arrived, she quickly jumped inside and pressed number one. Losing two precious minutes with the elevator, she sighed as it reached the bottom and walked hastily towards the alcove. Yet, when she stepped out of the building she was overwhelmed with the sight of the black classic Cadillac convertible parked out front. Her smile suddenly bloomed as she turned in that direction excited to see JC. However, as she drew closer, she noticed him eyeing a bypasser.

"Hello!" Tina shouted as she approached. "You see something you like?"

"Yeah," JC replied with a brief look of embarrassment.

"I can hook you up."

"Nah," he replied, "I've got a girl. Get in."

"Get in? Oh. −None of that pop the door for the lady mess tonight? No getting your butt out the car and opening my door?"

"I'm sorry," he jested as he popped the door, but Tina stood there unmoved. She crossed her arms and watched as JC quickly got out of the car and walked over. However, before he could get to her, she jumped in the car and slammed the door shut. He stopped in his tracks and looked over at her, though she didn't bother to look back at him. Instead, she glanced at his previous interest that was now halfway across the parking lot. JC walked back to the driver's side and opened the door only to find that

Tina had jumped back out of the car and slammed the door shut again.

"Oh, I forgot," Tina shouted, "You have a girl. ...How rude of me to plop myself in her seat. Let me go and catch my bus."

JC watched her walk off but appeared to be slightly aroused by her jealousy. She had a serious attitude and acted as if they were already an item, so JC smartly let Betty's top down revealing the backseat full of roses and loose rose petals that Tina obviously didn't see. He then put on some soft music and watched her stride across the parking lot towards the bus stop. He bumped his horn twice, but she kept walking. He then bumped the horn once and turned up the music. Tina stride slowed and then she turned and looked back at him. He motioned for her to return but she just stopped and placed her hands on her hips. JC walked over to her and took her bag and her hand.

"I came here for you. ...And I'm not leaving without you. ...You, Ms. Tina, are my girl."

"Whatever. You don't look at my ass like you looked at that other girl's ass," Tina sneered.

"Turn around and let me see what you're working with, baby."

"No!" Tina laughed as JC pulled her close and reassured her with a kiss.

"You made a scene so everyone would know you're with me, huh?"

"No," Tina chuckled, "I did that because you were being a dog."

"...A dog?" JC laughed, "Ruff, ruff, let me see ya booty."

They laughed and played as they walked back to the car. When Tina saw all the roses, she screamed and hugged him tightly. She walked over to the car and pulled out a single rose and held it to her chest as she looked back at him. By now, an audience had gathered, and Tina surely gave them something to see. She stepped close to JC and gave him a long passionate kiss. He aided her into the car and kissed her hand before he let it go. When they pulled off, a trail of yellow and red rose petals filled the air, and Tina's smile was tremendous. She leaned over and rewarded him with yet another kiss and eyed him attentively.

"How'd you know where I worked, Jonathan?"

"Your momma told me," he replied."

"What? You spoke to my mother."

"I met your mother."

"How?"

"I stopped by to check on you and let you know that your car wasn't gonna be ready for a while. I was gonna leave the truck there for you to drive, but before I could turn the engine off, your mom jumped from behind a bush like the Marines. 'Ronald, boy, get over here and help me with these Collards.' I was like whoa! Wrong guy, but she didn't care. All she wanted was the grass out of her garden."

"She put you to work?" Tina laughed.

"Yeah, and gave me some tomatoes to take home. ...But what was really funny was when she lectured me 'bout Lashunda."

"Oh, my God!"

"Yeah, had me feeling guilty 'bout something I didn't even do...'bout someone I don't even know. I'm gonna have to find this Lashunda and cash in on some of the things I've been accused of."

"You want her number?" Tina replied as she sat up in her seat.

JC laughed but quickly realized that the Lashunda topic was

not one to toy with and instinctively threw his arm around her shoulder and kissed her on the forehead.

They exited highway 20 and turned left onto Lake June Boulevard. As they passed Cooper Road, they entered an area that many consider a hustler's paradise. It was a twelve-block strip that had the biggest clubs, the fanciest restaurants and the greatest concentration of ill-gotten wealth in the region. A fair share of the businesses on Lake June had undisclosed ownership because many of the owners loved Lake June money but loathed the attention that came with Lake June activities.

Tina's eyes were full as they inched down the boulevard among the countless number of fancy vehicles that lined both sides of the road. She had never been out on Lake June after nightfall. It was far too dangerous. However, this was a typical Lake June night with hordes of people walking back and forth from car to car, club to club, and any combination of other things. The same Monday through Sunday, Lake June was always busy and swarming with every category of person you can think of: the poor, the rich, the hood-rich, the blacks, the whites, the Latinos, the Orientals and everyone in between.

Rose petals were still being caught by the wind and blown into the air behind them as they rolled down the strip. "Did y'all get married?" Someone yelled, and JC smiled and looked over into Tina's eyes.

"I have never thought of myself as the marrying type, but if I was to marry, it would be to someone like you." Tina didn't reply. She just smiled and kissed him softly on the cheek. Just then JC saw 'Wardo standing in front of a bar cleaning his nails with a pocketknife. JC made a left at the next side street and drove up the alley to Crimson Moon. Just as they pulled up to the dock, Tina noticed a couple getting it on next to the dumpster.

"Jonathan, look! They're screwing," she yelled, and JC simply laughed.

"Well, at least they're not shooting up."

"At least not yet," Tina replied as they both chuckled at the dual meaning of his statement.

JC let up the top on the convertible and lead Tina up the short stairwell and unlocked the door. A few more words and a kiss were shared between them as JC opened the door for her. As she stepped inside, she was grabbed from behind, and JC quickly went for his gun. In a matter of seconds, Tina was standing between the barrels of a Desert Eagle and a Colt Defender. Her skin grew pale as a tear rolled down her cheek and the arms around her neck grew tighter. Yet, as quickly as it all began, the guns lowered and the arm loosened around her neck. Then JC walked over and hugged his boy, happy to see him alive and well.

"So what's up, JC? Who's the broad?" Deuce said, in his usual distasteful manner.

"Her name is Tina, and she's not a broad. She's my girl," JC replied, as he pulled her to himself and wrapped his arms around her in an attempt to calm her down.

"Your girl?" Deuce continued, "Nigger, I thought you were boning Treasure. ...So, you saying I can get up on that now, cause that broad's fine? Well, both of these ho's fine, but I ain't too fond of this timid type. I like 'em feisty like that Treasure broad."

Deuce goes on talking, but JC pays him little mind. He just walks Tina into the office and shuts the door behind them. He then has someone bring her back a club soda and some chicken wings. They sat in the office and talked for some time. Deuce walked back into the club to harass someone else.

"So who the hell was that guy, anyway?" Tina questioned.

"That was Deuce."

"Deuce?"

"Yeah, he's a character. Sometimes you have to overlook his ignorance for the sake of his brilliance. He was shot in the shoulder the other night, so he's a little uptight now. Don't worry 'bout him. He's a pussycat."

"Shouldn't he be in bed somewhere resting?"

"Well, that's Deuce. He will be in bed somewhere within the next couple of hours, but I assure you he won't be resting."

"So do you know the owner of this place, too?"

"Yeah, I know him very well," JC jeers, "In fact, I am so at one with his vision that I manage this club almost precisely to his plans."

"Wow, he must pay you a lot to drive such nice cars and wear such nice clothes."

"Yeah," JC chuckled, "Let me show you around."

He grabbed Tina's hand and led her down a graffiti-covered hallway to a large reddish-orange door that had a large yellow smiley face and the words smile you're on camera painted on it. Tina sneered at the sight of it and replied, "Guess this is going to be my television début."

"Guess so," JC replied with a large smile on his face. "We'll be sure to catch every angle."

They entered the club just left of the bar and to the right of a large industrial stairwell that had been painted a dark shade of red to match the crimson hue of the walls and floors. There were not many people there. The club was less than half-full. The DJ played Zydeco music, and a few couples were out on the floor dancing but other than that, it was pretty calm. He stepped to the right toward the bar and ordered himself a whiskey sour.

"What would you like Ms. Tina?"

"I don't know. I'll try what you have."

"Make it two whiskey sours," he uttered to the bartender.

"Let me Guess," Tina followed, the bartender's the owner, and you're good friends with him too?"

"No," JC said with a big smile.

"The bartender is the bartender, and you're good friends with the owner."

"Whatever!" she said. "How'd you get this job? And where's your gun-happy friend?"

"Deuce? He's probably upstairs playing pool."

"I hate people like that. ...And what were you doing with a gun, Jonathan?"

"Whoa...slow down Ms. Tina. Sip your whiskey. You're getting crunk again." Tina downed the whiskey sour in a gulp and after the cringe and burn, started back up where she had left off. JC quickly handed her a fresh drink and ordered another.

The two of them strolled along the wall speaking to people here and there. He introduced Tina to the DJ and then they walked up the stairwell to the second floor. The second level was known as The Player's Floor because there was nothing but games played there. It had eight mahogany red-felt pool tables, four aligned in a row on each side of the room. The center of the room had ten round mahogany tables with matching chairs that were set aside for card and domino games. Along each wall were various types of video games and pinball machines. Deuce was sitting at one of the center tables playing poker. His eyes glanced over at Tina and then back at his hand. JC was offered a hand in a domino game but courteously passed. He led Tina back to the stairwell and up to the third floor. This floor was closed to the public; Tina marveled at the large mahogany table in the center of the room. It had about eighteen matching plush leather chairs surrounding it. Each side of the room was lined with empty offices. JC took Tina to the office on the far left side of the room. Sync was sitting inside it surrounded by electronic equipment and about twenty monitors.

"Wow!" Tina uttered when she stepped inside. "You must see everything from up here."

"What's up Sync," JC said as they shook hands. "This is my girl, Tina. I was just showing her around."

"Hi, Tina. Nice meeting you," Sync said, as he shook her hand.

"What's going on?" JC asks.

"Not much, except your boy Deuce cheating at the poker table."

"I'd be more surprised to know that he wasn't?" JC replied. Then both of them laughed.

"Do you trust him?" Sync asked.

"Yeah, Deuce is alright..."

Sync released the controls and leaned back in his seat noting the manner in which Deuce held his cards. He knew Sync was watching, which meant that he also knew about the hidden cameras that were recently installed. Sync looked over at JC and asked again, "You trust him?"

"Hell no," Tina interjects, "He's a gun-happy thug, he's ugly, and he's down there cheating. I don't trust him. I think you should have him arrested."

Sync and JC laughed, knowing that she had no idea of what was going on. Sync knew Deuce could carry out a task if given, but what he was really asking was how loyal was Deuce? What was the likeliness that he would become a traitor? How much pressure could he stand, and foremost, could he move past his spontaneous ways? JC stared at Deuce for a moment through the monitor, knowing now exactly what sync was asking. He watched him scratch his left hand with his right and switch a seven for an Ace that he had up his sleeve. Deuce was indeed a master of deception, but he had yet to be tested to the degree that would comfort The Reaper. JC rubbed his chin as if he was in deep thought and said "Go down there and tell him he has a call in the office, and when he gets down there, shut the door and tell him what's expected of him. If he has any questions, have him call me. I'll be home."

"Alright bro," Sync replied, "Hope to see you again sometime, Ms. Tina."

"Yeah, same here," Tina replied as she got up from her seat and grasped JC's hand.

He existed from the opposite stairwell not wanting to bump into anyone else on the way out. When they got to the bottom floor, they exited the stairwell next to the dance floor and without warning someone runs up to them screaming.

"Tina! Girl, how are you doing? Is this your new boyfriend? He's cute. Guess what, girl? I'm pregnant."

"By who?" Tina replied.

"Well uh, I think its Chad because he just got a new car and he's fine, girl."

"You don't know who your baby's daddy is?" Tina asked.

"I do. It's Chad or Chris. I don't think its Reginald because we don't do it that much, but it's so good to see you. Girl, where you been? I hear you going to college?"

"Yeah, Well. Nice seeing you, Janice. Good luck with that baby, girl. I gotta go!"

"See ya, girl. ...You take care of that man."

"Yeah, Bye!"

JC and Tina nearly sprinted through the club and back to the car. They laughed and joked about everything that had happened in the small amount of time since she had left work. She handled it all well, and JC was most impressed.

When they got to the car, JC helped her in, as was their custom, and kissed her gently before he shut the door. As they pulled off, he asked her about Janice. Tina didn't have much to say other than she had tutored her in math a couple of times. Janice, she said, didn't want much out of life but to find a man who would take care of her. JC laughed.

"That seems to be a lot of peoples' problem. They want someone to do for them. ...I don't want anybody to do for me. I want to be independent, to have my own thang. I wanna wake up in the morning and know that whether I get up or not, my money is making me more money. I know you worry about the things I do, but they're a means to an end. The means to my independence.... My freedom." Tina didn't reply. She simply snuggled close to him and laid her head on his shoulder.

They arrived at her house rather late. JC's Suburban was parked out front. He handed her the keys as she exited the car.

"I don't want my truck looking like your car, so you drive slowly and safely."

"I don't wanna drive that," Tina replied, "I wanna drive the Cadillac."

"Betty? Hell no! You can drive the truck. No man wheels my baby."

"I'm not a man. ...and I thought I was your baby?"

"Whatever, man. I filled up the tank so you should be ok. I'll be back to see you on Saturday afternoon."

"I have to work Saturday."

"Your job is crazy. Nobody should have to work weekends."

"I can see you Saturday evening around six," Tina said.

"Alright then. Take care of my truck," he said as they reached the top of the porch. "Drive slowly and safely."

Tina laughed as he kissed her on the forehead and trotted down the steps back to the car. When she entered the house, she was surprised to see her mother waiting.

"That Ronald's a fine young man. He gon' let you drive his daddy's truck to work, baby?"

"Momma Ronald's gone. That's Jonathan."

"Jonathan?"

"Yeah, He's my new boyfriend."

"I don't understand, girl. What happened to Ronald? He was a fine young man."

"No Momma. Ronald was a pig."

"...But he was here helping me with my Azaleas today."

"No. That was Jonathan that helped you in the garden today. He helped you pull the grass from between the collard greens, and you gave him some tomatoes to take home. That was Jonathan."

"Jonathan?"

"Yes."

"Well, how many boyfriends you got, baby?"

"Momma? Just one!" Tina said as she laughed at her mother's sorting of the situation.

CHAPTER SEVEN

Four in the morning, while JC and Tina were asleep in their humble homes, there was a knock at Deuce's door. However, he didn't answer. Treasure waited several minutes before knocking again, but even then, there wasn't an answer. She walked over to his car and rubbed her hand across the hood and saw that it was warm. She then reached into her purse and pulled out two metal tools and within seconds, picked the lock and entered the house.

All the lights were off, but the front rooms were sufficiently lit by the outdoor lights. She walked around the living room. It was nice considering its owner. She took special notice of the bong in the corner next to the recliner. It was huge but quite simple in design. It had a solid burnt-orange colored glass bowl, shiny copper-colored fittings and was almost half-full of water. She walked into the kitchen, then through the dining room and on to the hallway leading to the bedrooms where she was met by an odor of a different type. The sound of grunts reverberated amongst a rhythmic banging. She smiled as she approached a half-opened door. Deuce was hard at work on Janice. Her back was heavily arched as she buried her face in the pillows and absorbed his steady thrusts.

Treasure opened the door and walked in unnoticed and had a seat in the chair next to the dresser. Several minutes passed before Deuce came to a stop and pulled Janice's rear-end up firmly against him and let out a thunderous grunt of his own. He then pushed her flat onto the bed and pulled off his condom and flung it on her. "Sorry bitch!" he yelled, as he reached onto the floor and grabbed a bottle of gin and took a large manly gulp. He stood up next to the bed and chugged down another. Just as he lowered the bottle, he noticed Treasure's smiling face. He spat the gin from his mouth and yelled, "What the hell?" He hurried over to her and asked, "How you get up in here?"

"The door was open," Treasure retorted.

"That door wasn't open!"

"Then how did I get in, Deuce?"

He just stood there for a minute and glanced toward the door and then back at Treasure. Janice had covered herself in the blankets, and Deuce ran over there and snatched them off of her.

"What you doing? Get up! Get yo ass dressed," he shouted.

"Why you yelling at me and who's that?" "Shut up and get dressed."

"Deuce!"

"Shut up I said and get yo ass dressed.

Treasure watched as if she was at a live play, still smiling as the drama built. He looked back at Treasure with a measure of suspicion and walked toward her. "What you want! Some dick?"

"No," she said. "We need to get up on some money."

"Some money?" Deuce questioned, as he started to dress.

"Yeah, Greenbacks."

Deuce was not suspecting her, and he knew she did not care for him, so he was silent for the few minutes it took him to gather his clothes. Janice kept hitting him behind the head asking who Treasure was, why she was there and where they were going. Deuce kept pushing her away and ignoring her punches. He stood up and took another long swig of his gin before he put on his pants. Janice yelled and screamed constantly, but Deuce paid her little mind. He hasted over to Treasure as she stood from her chair.

"What kind o' money you talking?"

"Handle your business, Deuce. I'll be outside."

"What business? ...This broad?" Deuce asked as he pointed back at Janice. "She ain't nothing." He grabbed his shirt and began to put it on. "I met her at the club... running her mouth with a bunch o' South Dallas broads... simple-minded hoes." Janice then threw a shoe at him but missed.

"Who you calling simple?" she yelled, "...You can't be disrespecting me like I ain't nobody. You da one who ain't shit!"

"Shut up!" Deuce countered. "...You dressed? ...Huh! ...Hurry up and gitcho stuff together and get the hell up out o' here!" Then almost immediately, he turned back to Treasure. "...So what you got in mind?"

"...Collecting on our money and shaking things up a 'lil, like the other day."

"Ha! A'ight then," he smirked, "...and once we're done?"

"Look out, Deuce."

"Oh, you gon gimme dat?"

"No, but you'd better turn around." Just then another shoe made contact with the back of his head, and he quickly spun around and snatched the shoe from the floor and threw it back at Janice. She tried to block it, but it hit her in the face. Her eye puffed-up almost instantly and turned a blackish blue. She fell to the floor holding her face and cowered as he approached her. Treasure exited the apartment and got back in her car.

A few moments later Deuce came out of the house dragging Janice by the hair. She screamed frantically as he repeatedly threw her about and grabbed her again before she could run away. After humiliating her in a way she couldn't have known possible, he threw her down the steps and stood over her yelling countless insults. It was only after the honk of Treasure's horn that he finally walked back up the porch and locked the door.

He pulled his car into the garage and walked back to Treasure's car. Treasure was lighting a joint as he approached. Janice ran up behind him and hit him in his wounded shoulder.

"Who's gonna take me home?"

Deuce backhanded her, blackening her other eye and then threw a $50 bill at her.

"Consider this a tip," he replied, "...and catch yo ass a cab."

Treasure chuckled at his remark and shifted the car into reverse. She sped out the driveway as if she was driving forward, and whipped the car around quickly and burned off. Deuce held on tight as they made their rounds. One after the other, everything went perfectly. No one shorted them their cash, and everyone who didn't have the remaining cash still had the product, so there was no foul. After they left the last crack house, Deuce asked her to stop at Waffle House so they could get breakfast. She gladly obliged, and when they arrived, she darted for a booth at the end of the counter.

Deuce placed his order and watched Treasure as she placed hers. The waitress hung on her every word as Treasure complimented her and conned her into giving them their meal almost free. Deuce cocked his head to one side and looked into

Treasure's eyes.

"What color are your eyes?" He asked, but she continued to speak with the waitress while their order was being made. "What color are your eyes?" He asked again.

"What difference does it make?"

"I like 'em."

"Excuse me," Treasure says to the waitress, and then leans over the table towards Deuce. "Come here, Deuce." He leaned over as if he expected a kiss as she leaned toward him and gently cupped the back of his head with her left hand and rubbed the smoothness of his skin. "I like you because you're straight up, but, using your words, I'm not one of them simple-minded South Dallas broads you're used to. You see, I always have a hand on my piece, and I have no problem shooting you in the ass."

Deuce quickly pulled away and looked intensely at her and the waitress, who laughed freely.

"You're some sick bitches," he snapped.

"No sicker than you," the waitress opposed.

"You just go get my food!" Deuce snapped.

Treasure smiled at him as his eye's settled back on her.

"What? Y'all some bull-daggers or somp'n?" He asked.

"No, she's just someone I know."

"...From where?"

"...Not your business."

"...So what's your connection?"

"Again, not your business."

"So what, now we have secrets?"

"Deuce, did that shoe knock the sense outta yo head? We ain't a couple. We ain't even friends. We're working together for a time. Yo thang is yo thang, and my thang is mine. Get over it, man, you blowing my high."

"Speaking 'o high, where'd you get that weed."

"Where'd you get your pistol?"

"None of yo business, answer the question."

"My answer's pointed at your balls." He quickly jumped from his seat and walked over to the counter and sat down.

"That broad's crazy," he said under his breath. Then Treasure motioned for him to come back. He glanced at her but didn't move. She then got up and walked over to him and put her arm around his neck and reached down to his chest. Her chest pressed gently against his back, and she leaned her head over and kissed him on the cheek. He leaned his head to the side as if to say he wasn't fazed by her action, but his mere nature gave him away. She laid her pistol in his lap.

"Let's say this is an act of goodwill," she whispered.

"Let's say you're the craziest broad ever," he said. "Everyone knows your crazy ass packs two pistols."

She chuckled and grabbed a seat next to him. He put the pistol under his shirt and in-between his belt and pants. The waitress then placed their plates in front of them, and they began to eat. Not another word was spoken until they got back into the car. It was almost ten o'clock then.

Deuce pulled out Treasure's pistol as they pulled up into his driveway. Just as he was handing it to her, he noticed the house's front windows had been broken. He jumped out of the car before it came to a stop. He tripped as he rushed up the driveway. He marched completely around the house and realized that all of his windows had been broken. Janice obviously got her revenge and Deuce was enraged.

"That bitch!" he yelled at the top of his lungs, "We gotta go find her."

"For what?" Treasure replied.

"For jacking up my house!"

"You jacked up her face and stomped on her pride. I'd say yall 'bout even. Besides, I got something to do before the meeting."

"What meeting?"

"Nothing, Deuce," she exclaimed as she backed out the driveway.

"What meeting?" He yelled.

"Good luck with the house thang," she uttered. "See ya!"

"Hey! Hey!" Deuce yelled as she pulled away, "What meeting?"

Deuce could only stand there as she drove off, leaving him to deal with his situation alone. He grimaced as he walked back to the house and sat down in his recliner, and after a brief pause, he casually reached into a nearby drawer. He felt around purposefully for a minute and then jumped up and pulled the drawer all the way out. "What?" He yelled in disgust and pulled out the other drawers. "Dammit! I knew that was my weed that broad was smoking. Nobody got that kind o' Jane 'round here." He threw his lighter to the floor and walked to his bedroom mumbling words of discontent. However, when he stepped into his closet he, pulled back the carpet, lifted a floorboard, pulled out a pound of Tai weed and took about two ounces from it. The remaining weed, the floorboard, and carpet were then put back in place. Deep thought seemed to have come over him as he walked back into the living room, broke down his weed and rolled up about twenty joints. Half of them he put in a Ziploc bag and placed some in his shirt pocket and the other half he threw back in the weed bag and placed in the drawer next to the recliner. The fattest joint, however, was placed between his lips and lit and, as was his custom, the mighty tokes were washed down with gin. He swept up the broken glass as he indulged, and when he filled his last dustpan with glass, he began to laugh. "Treasure," he said audibly. "Huh! That broad's crazy." He chuckled some more and then went and freshened up.

After a shower and more gin, he got dressed and went to speak to a crack-fiend about fixing his windows. Once they agreed on a deal, the man set off to find Deuce's new windows.

It was almost 2:00 pm, now, so Deuce made haste towards Lake June seeming extremely concerned about something, squirming in his seat as he drove. When he exited Jim Miller Boulevard, he stopped by a friend's house a couple of blocks from one of JC's crack houses and hung out about twenty minutes before he continued on. It was obvious that this was not the typical Lake June trip by the route Deuce took. He drove out of his way to avoid being seen; and stopped at an apartment complex two blocks up from Crimson Moon and then walked back down to the club.

There were two cars parked in Crimson's parking lot, so Deuce subtly moved to the rear of the building and let himself in. He scurried up the stairs unnoticed and hid in the third floor supply closet. It was obvious that his intention was to listen in on JC's meeting and get an idea of what all JC had going on and why it was so covert. However, two and a half hours would pass before anyone would show up.

Treasure and Sync were the first ones to enter, and shortly after, JC and Gimme came in. JC grimaced at the music playing through the house speakers and went over to the bar and changed the music to something a little more upbeat, a little more appropriate. As Treasure and Sync grooved to the O'Jays', "For the Love of Money," Scratch rolled in with a large duffle bag in her lap. Mario and six others followed in close behind her. This was the twelve men and women that made up The Reaper, all in one place at one time. Scratch sat at the head of the table with JC sitting to her right and Treasure, Sync and Mario to her left. Everyone else was seated casually around the large mahogany table, kicked back in the leather chairs. JC was staring at the ceiling with his hands clasped together over his chest when the music stopped. Scratch slung the duffle bag onto the table, and it slid close to the center before stopping. A bundle of money fell out onto the table. It was several stacks of hundreds, fifties, and twenties wrapped in cellophane and taped together with duct tape. Everyone was silent as Mario sat up and grabbed the loose bundle and turned it in his hands.

"That's $564,980," Scratch yelled, "so everybody's cut is $47,080. I kept the change, so I don't wanna hear no mess later 'bout calculations." Everybody laughed, and Mario tossed each person their $47,080 bundle. Deuce squirmed as he tried to listen attentively through the small opening at the bottom of the door.

"It seemed like it was more than this," Mario exclaimed. "This is one sorry ass bag. I counted at least three of these hoes going into the truck. ...You keeping a lot of change, Scratch."

"...So, who you calling a liar?" JC abruptly interrupted. "You the accountant now?" he shouted.

"Nah man, I'm just saying..."

"Saying what? Huh! Saying what?" JC yelled as he rose from his seat. "I run this...irrevocably, inequitably and uncontestedly! If you got somethin' to say, you say it to me! I set the payout!"

Just then the door burst open, and Deuce walked in with his gun drawn, but down at his side. Almost instantly eight of the twelve were standing around the table with their guns drawn. JC quickly lifted his hand as if to keep anyone from firing. Deuce lowered himself and placed his pistol on the floor and began to speak.

"JC…"

"Shut up!" JC shouted. "What you doing here?"

"I came to…"

"Shut the hell up!" JC yelled as he walked towards Deuce and kicked the gun out of his reach. "Get on your knees, punk!" Deuce places his hands on his head and kneels down to his knees. Treasure moved towards Deuce with her gun pointed at his head and kicked him in the chest. "Mario!" JC yelled. "Bring your punk ass over here, too." Just then the man next to Mario placed a sawed-off shotgun up to his throat.

"Move it, boss," the man whispered to Mario, and Mario gladly sidestepped his chair and lowered himself to his knees next to Deuce.

"Two idiots," JC yelled, "that don't know why they're here, messing up something beautiful. I call the shots, you understand me? I RUN THIS…not Deuce, not Mario or anyone else. I decide how things are financed. I decide what jobs get done and what jobs don't. I've supported both of you, and both of you have let me down a hundred times and I ain't shot either of your asses yet. I must be stupid, huh?"

The room was silent. JC then bent over and asked Deuce what he saw in the room, and Deuce replied, "Nothing, J, man, I don't see nothing."

"Good answer," JC followed. "Who do you see in this room, Deuce?"

"I don't see nobody, J."

"Good! This brotha has all the right answers today. Get up!" Deuce stammered to his feet, and JC asked, "How you gone repay me for ya goof-up, Deuce?

"I'll do your next job for free and you can still split it twelve ways like I wasn't even involved." JC looked attentively at Deuce.

"You ain't part of my crew. Why would I wanna trust you like that for?"

"JC, man you know you can trust me, man. I've kept the streets tight, and I haven't cheated you one red cent, man."

"Treasure," JC asked. "How's my money on Eden Valley."

"It's tight."

"And Lawton Drive?"

"Tight..."

"And the rest of them?"

"They're all tight."

"Deuce, sit your ass at the table. I got something for you to do, but you best to remember, you ain't part of my crew. You understand that?"

"Yeah. I got it."

"Mario, get your ass up too," JC said, as he watched Deuce seat himself at the table. "Don't jerk with me, okay? I got a mind to shoot your ass right here, you ungrateful motherfucker. You got one more time. One... Now, go sit yo' punk ass down."

Moments later, with everyone seated at the table, JC and Sync began to brief everyone on the next gig. Once the assignments were given, and all the rules and deadlines were determined, the table was cleared, and several men walked in pushing cloth covered carts. The music came back on, and the carts were uncovered revealing an entire buffet of food. Deuce walked pass Gimme and asked, "What the hell you doing here?" But Gimme never acknowledged the fact that Deuce spoke. He simply rolled over to the carts and grabbed him a plate. Deuce attempted to follow, but JC stopped him in his tracks.

"The playing field has changed, Deuce," JC remarked. "Each person here is a professional, a master at what they do and you're no different. This gig will take several weeks of planning, so you'll have a little time, but you have to deliver what we need as soon as possible."

"Yeah, man. I got it but keep that man-bitch away from me."

"Man-bitch?"

"Yeah, Treasure. That broad's been a thorn in my side since we met."

JC laughed. "Yeah, it's done, but it's time for you to go."

"Go? Man, I'm finna get me some of this food."

"No, you're not," JC said calmly. "You haven't earned the right to share in our spoils yet. Get you a burger down the street somewhere."

Deuce then gives JC an intense stare and Treasure walks up from behind JC and places her hand on his shoulder.

"Everything Ok?" she asked.

"Is everything ok, Deuce?" JC asked.

"Yeah," Deuce said as he walked off.

The evening was still young, but all that food did make Deuce hungry, so he hurried on to Caribbean Nites Bar & Grill. The same Rasta met him at the door as last time and frisked him for weapons. He didn't find any weapons on Deuce, but he did find the weed. Deuce simply smiled and lifted it from the Rasta's hands.

"You hook up the jerk chicken, and I'll hook up the smokes."

"No problem, Mon," the Rasta replied, and a small framed woman with long thick locks led Deuce to his table and gave him a beer. Several minutes later the same woman brought him jerk chicken.

"You trying to entice me with that sexy ass walk of yours?" Deuce asked.

"It's me Nach'ral wok, Mon," she replied, "You be needing

another beer?"

"Yeah, and them two chicken legs of yours."

"Me not on dah menu, love," she answered as she emptied his ashtray into a nearby trashcan, "and if me was, you couldn't afford me, Mon."

Deuce smiled at her quick wit and watched attentively as she walked away, disappearing into the smoke and darkness. Deuce ate about half of his meal before the Rasta walked up to the table.

"You got company," he stated. Deuce got up and walked to the door, and Mario was standing there between two heavily armed Rastas. "What you want?" He asked.

"I just want to talk with you for a minute."

"...'bout what?"

"...About a way to get more money."

"I'm listening."

"Well, can we sit down and talk somewhere?"

Deuce motioned for the Rastas to let Mario in, and they allowed him to walk back to Deuce's table and have a seat. One of the Rastas stood behind Mario with an Uzi in his hands the entire time they were there.

"What you want, man?" Deuce asked impatiently.

"I wanna talk to you man-to-man about what happened today."

Deuce took a bite of his chicken and nodded his head. "I'm listening, talk!"

"JC's a hothead, man. He comes up with all these elaborate schemes and doesn't care who gets hurt. He just wants the money."

"I'm listening," Deuce replied after he took another bite of his chicken.

"I normally wouldn't come at you like this, but I see that you're as hungry as I am, and he disrespects us both the same."

"So what you want to do, take out JC?"

"No, I just wanna be able to maximize on my cut," Mario went on "Think about it, JC doesn't know how much money we will get in PGA. That's another drug dealer we're robbing and not to mention that practically all the residents are gang members. We will be the ones moving the money from PGA to the truck at Big Town Mall. Why can't we take a cut before we drop it off to Xavier? Hell! Why can't we just crank it up ourselves? You know everything JC knows and more. Besides, he's too flamboyant. Sooner or later Antonio's gonna have him killed, and then what?"

"Why would Antonio care," Deuce asked. "What I see, Antonio's business benefits from JC's activities. All JC's stuff does is eliminate Antonio's competition."

"No, Deuce, you have to see the big picture," Mario explained. "Antonio's getting old. Sooner or later his nephew, 'Wardo, will take over, and he will need someone to make an example of. Who better than JC? Why do you think JC gets off so much easier than others? Antonio's keeping him around for a reason, but even if he does knock JC off, that'll only open up the streets for people like us, the go-getters."

"How do you know all this stuff you coming to me with?"

"I have my means. Stick with me and we will get rich fast benefiting off of JC's demise."

Deuce looked down and twirled the bottom of his empty beer bottle on the table and slowly looked up at Mario. "This is the best damn jerk chicken in the world," he solemnly uttered.

"I bet it is," Mario smiled. "Next time, I will have to have a bite."

Mario then arose from his seat and was escorted to the door by the Rastas. Moments later the Rasta that worked the door came to Deuce's table.

"We no won no trouble," he said. "When you bring it to us, den we bring it bok to you."

"Yeah, I know," Deuce said dejectedly.

"Why you won war with JC?" the Rasta continued. "When great men war, dem kill more den enemy. Dem kill friends. Dem kill families. Dem kill community. When you war with JC, you no more welcome here. You eat at Colonel Kentucky, for the war you won bring, will overrun the whole of Lake June. We no won dat war."

"Yeah, Kevin, man, I'll keep that in mind...I'll keep it all in mind," Deuce replied.

CHAPTER EIGHT

The following day was Juneteenth, a true Juneteenth some said because it was the 19th of June and on the weekend. The whole state of Texas smelled of barbecue that day and the citywide events were numerous.

JC held a get-together at his house, and he and Xavier ran the pit. Everyone was supposed to bring a dish but of course, everyone didn't. Yet, there was more than enough food with all that had been brought. Someone there was a big Stevie Wonder fan because his songs rang out so frequently from JC's four three-foot tall speakers that Stevie Wonder himself would've asked them to change the CD. It was nice gathering, however, and everyone seemed to find themselves a small group within the group to hang around with.

Scratch was pulled to the table with Sync and Treasure while Mario and few others were out back shooting dice. JC mingled in and out the crowd touching every person there in some small way, being as hospitable as he knew how.

Gimme was listening to the basketball game on a small handheld radio that he had pressed up against his ear when

Deuce walked through the front door. Being that Gimme's back was to the door, he wasn't aware of who entered, especially, since people had been coming in and out of it all day; stopping by for food, to say hello, what's up and so on. It was like a family reunion there with so many people packed into that small space in Oakcliff.

As Deuce passed by Gimme, he slapped the radio from his hand and kicked it as it hit the floor. A young lady who was standing nearby saw what Deuce had done and began to yell at him as he entered the kitchen.

She then gathered up the batteries, put them back into the radio and handed it back to Gimme. The two of them then began their own conversation, aside from everyone else.

Later that evening, Deuce made his way back into the living room and sat down in front of the television with a plate of barbecue and potato salad. JC and Xavier were seated across from him, on the couch, talking about the restaurant.

"How 'bout $250,000?" Xavier asked.

"Why you think I wanna sell my half of the restaurant?"

"You never were interested in that restaurant you just needed a way to clean up some cash. You have other businesses that can do that for you now. I just wanna rest knowing that my dream is secure."

"Secure? You think I'm gone mess up or something?"

"Nah man, you know what I'm saying. Moms-and-nem are proud of us right now, and I want it to stay like that. Man, I was busted when we got started, and you fronted a hell-of-a-lot cash to make this happen. I ain't messing with that. Hell, I owe you for the part I own, but I want to do something special."

"Scratch!" JC yelled, and in a matter of seconds, she rolled into the room.

"Yeah!" She replied roughly.

"I wanna sign the entire restaurant over to Xavier. He's buying me out for $250,000."

"Alright," she replied.

"Where's the money?"

"Let's just say it's already paid."

"Okay, don't be throwing a hissy when the books are all jacked up."

Everyone laughed at her response, but Deuce.

"I've been saving for this moment forever, man," said Xavier.

"I'll get the money to you by Wednesday."

"I'm for real, man," JC replied, "You've done more for me and my sanity than $250,000 can ever do. We're square."

"You sure?" "Yeah, man. Go ahead; get some of them drinks in ya before they're all gone."

"Yeah, I'll do that," Xavier got up and walked into the kitchen.

"Let me get this straight," Deuce stated as he bit into a spare rib. "We owe Antonio $100,000 that we don't have, and you gon' give Xavier a whole restaurant?"

"Yeah."

"And he owes you $250,000 that you're gone forgive?"

"Yeah."

"Well, since you being Santa Claus, what do you have for a brotha like me?"

"Short patience... I take care of them that take care of me Xavier took a bullet for me. Did you know that? He was there for me before all this existed and is still with me now. You can't buy that kind of loyalty, Deuce. The problem is Xavier was never supposed to be part of this. I led him out into the streets and despite what he thinks is the reason I purchased the restaurant, I bought it to get him off the streets, a way of righting my wrong with God. Shiiiit, he likes to cook. It's his passion. It's time that he gets outta the game for good, and this will finally ensure that."

"So who's gonna take that brotha's spot?" Deuce retorted.

"That's not your concern. "Just do what we agreed. Now, I'm 'bout to get me some more of this pie."

Just as JC exited, Mario entered. He was grinning from ear to ear but didn't say a word. Making eye contact with Deuce was enough. Deuce subtly gave him a nod and met him outside by the cars.

"What's up, Deuce?" Mario said with a shrewd smile.

"...That fool's crazy."

"...Like I told ya."

"Xavier owes him $250,000, and he's gone forgive it all! ...Gone tell me some stuff 'bout Xavier taking a bullet for him. My spot's gone be shut down if I don't get that stuff from Antonio, and he ain't doing nothing until JC pays that motherfuckin' money."

"How long he give him to pay it back?"

"He should've paid up yesterday, but I ain't heard nothing 'bout it."

"Hmm. Let's get out of here, man," Mario said as he looked back at the house.

"Yeah, meet me at Johnnie's in an hour," Deuce told him.

"Yeah. Alright, I'll do that."

An hour later Mario showed up at Johnnie's, just as instructed. He looked around for Deuce but didn't find him, so he sat at the bar and had a few beers. After some time had passed, he looked up at the clock and noticed the time. It was eight pm, an hour past the time they were supposed to meet, so he decided to leave. As he made it back to his truck, he noticed

Deuce's car parked at the edge of the parking lot. Shattered glass was everywhere. The driver's door was open, and the keys were still in the ignition. Mario looked inside the car and saw Deuce's pistol wedged between the seats and a half-spilt pint of gin on the floor. He immediately went back into the pool hall and called JC and told him what he had seen.

When he went back outside to the car, he saw Deuce tied up on the ground. He hurried over to assist him but noticed a police car turning the corner a block up, so he kneeled down and hid between the cars. The officer turned on his flashers when he noticed that someone was lying on the ground and hurried up into the parking lot. However, once he saw who it was, he turned the flashers off, rolled down his window and laughed coldly. The officer never got out of the car. He simply said a few things to someone over the radio, rolled up his window and drove off.

Once the officer was well enough up the block, Mario came over and cut the cords off of Deuce's legs and hands.

"What happened to you man!" He asked as he helped Deuce to his feet. Deuce didn't say a word. He just took a swing at Mario and fell back to the ground. Mario helped him up again, and Deuce leaned against his car for several minutes. His face had swollen on both sides from the assaults of Antonio's spoon. "Hey! Deuce! You alright, man?" Mario asked, "You need to go to the hospital?"

Deuce didn't answer. He just moved the glass from the seat with his hand and sat down in the car.

"Get in," Deuce responded, and Mario walked to the other side and got in. By that time, Deuce had grabbed his pistol and was holding it firmly in his hand.

"What's going on?" Mario continued.

"With what?" Mario replied, "You think I had something to do with this?"

"What's going on between you, JC and Antonio?"

"Antonio did this?"

"Answer the question!"

"What! Who the hell you think you're talking to...some broad? Man, I don't know you..."

Deuce leaned his head back against the headrest and closed his eyes. "...But you know me well enough to do your own dirt with. ...You're back and forth, brotha. One moment you wanna get together and scam JC. The next, you don't know who the hell I am or what's happening." He sat up in his seat and leaned over to Mario. "I need to know what's going on and I need to know it tonight. Who's screwing who? ...Are you working with Antonio to set up JC? Are you working with JC to set me up? Somebody is gonna straighten some stuff up with me tonight."

"...Deuce," Mario jeered; as he perused the surrounding area, "JC doesn't trust you. We all know that. He keeps you close just in case..."

"In case of what?"

"In case he ever needs a fall guy."

"What?"

"Man, JC doesn't trust me either. You think I don't know he had you go through that whole charade Tuesday so that he could get you close to me; so that he can see if I'm the one leaking information to Antonio? I already know. He used you because you're expendable. I wouldn't be surprised if we were both being set up."

Deuce paused before he responded. "...Sync pulled me aside at the club the other day and told me they had a job for me. I laughed it off at first because I didn't know Sync was that deep. He told me when the meeting would be and what I was supposed to do. Then he called JC and handed me the phone. He said he wanted me to get close to you and find out what connections you had with Antonio. A hell-of-a-lot more happened than I expected, though. I wasn't expecting to be on my knees with a pistol to my head, but I just played along, hoping he remembered that he told me to be there." They each chuckled.

"I couldn't tell for sure," Mario replied, "but, then, I wasn't expecting to be on my knees either." They again laughed lightly. "...but that's the kind of craziness I was talking 'bout."

They were silent for a moment and then Deuce continued. "Antonio jumped me tonight. He says JC works with me and not me with him."

"...So he wants you to pay him?"

"Yeah!"

"Psst...How does that happen?"

"I don't know, but if Antonio wants to crown me king, then I'ma be a motherfuckin' king."

"What do you mean?" "I know how I can get the money in a couple of days."

"How's that?"

"Robin Hood, baby! ...Robin Hood."

CHAPTER NINE

JC's alarm went off at 8 am. He stared at it for several minutes before he mustered up the will and energy to get up, walk over to his dresser and turned it off. He leaned against the dresser for a moment rubbing his eyes before he went to the bathroom and washed his face and brushed his teeth. Then, staring into the mirror, he rubbed his chin and rendered a brief smile. It was Sunday morning and he was going to church. He shaved and showered and thumbed through his suits before settling on a medium grey suit with subtle pinstriping. Along with it, he chose a light blue shirt and a blue and grey diagonally-striped tie. He looked good and somewhat sharper and more distinguished in a suit and tie.

Once dressed, he grabbed the Gideon Bible he acquired from Dallas County jail a few years prior and set off to Pleasant Grove. When he arrived at Houghton Road and Creekside Drive, he slowly turned into the parking lot of The Holy Tabernacle Church of Pleasant Grove. It was a large church as neighborhood churches go. It had a tall roof with a white steeple on top. The walls seemed tall as well with its narrow purple tinted windows.

Unlike some of the other churches in the neighborhood, Reverend Liverpool kept the lawn meticulously manicured.

JC walked up the steps holding his bible in his right hand and his stomach with his left. The usher at the door greeted him and handed him a program. There was a small section between the entrance and the sanctuary that had the women's restroom to the right and the men's to the left. An usher there then led him and another family into the sanctuary and sat them in their respective Sunday school classes.

A big man with a puffy gray beard and matching hairdo taught JC's class. He seemed excited about the lesson he was teaching, but JC's attention was immediately drawn to the woman who sat two rows up. He could only see the back of her head from where he was seated, but he knew it was Tina. She had on a long taupe dress with white flower designs in it. Her hair was tied up in a bun and she wore a matching pearl-like necklace and earring set. JC was looking in her direction admiring his tiny angle of her the entire service, then just prior to dismissal, the teacher asked everyone stand and tell the class what they learned. Some of the people discussed the faith Moses had in God. Some others discussed issues surrounding the plagues or Pharaoh's stubbornness, but when they got to JC, he stood up and stated, "Jesus wept." Everyone laughed except the Sunday school teacher who began to bark at JC about the importance of the scriptures, but he just stood there with a smile on his face gazing deep into Tina's eyes. All he could hear was the sweet sound of her voice in his head.

"Hey! Hey! Young man, are you listening?" the Sunday school teacher asked.

JC looked up and replied, "Yes sir! ...And all that stuff you said 'bout Pharaoh parting the Red Sea, is pretty interesting." The class laughed all the more. JC took a seat there next to Tina.

When the class was finally dismissed, JC turned to Tina and opened his arms to hug her, but she stopped him and shook his hand.

"We're in church, Jonathan."

"It's alright. God knows me."

"Yeah, but judging by your responses today, you don't know much of him."

"Oh, it's like that?"

"Yeah!" Tina responded with a big smile on her face, "Let's go see Mom."

Tina then grabbed JC's hand and led him through the crowd to her mother and introduced them.

"Momma! I want you to meet somebody," Tina said excitable.

"Who baby?"

"This is my friend Jonathan: the guy who helped you in the garden the other day."

"Hi Jonathan," her mother replied, "You look different."

"...remember you thought he was Ronald, the other day?" Tina continued.

"I knew it wasn't Ronald. Ronald is good looking," her mother retorted, "but he can't garden worth-a-damn."

"Momma! We're in church," Tina replied.

"I know where we are lil girl," her mother continued, "but look-a-here, Jonathan. That's yo name, right?"

"Yes mama," JC answered.

"The only hoe 'round here is the one I put in yo hand the other day. Now you keep yo ass as straight as that row of azaleas you planted and we'll be ok. You got that?"

"Yes mama, JC replied and then looked at Tina.

"Don't look at her look at me! You hear me?

"Yes."

"Good. Now, come sit next to me... both of you."

JC hadn't been talked to like that by anyone other than his mother in quite some time, but he undoubtedly understood her. Her mannerisms were a lot like those of his mother so in the end he just sat there at her right while Tina graced her left.

The service was long and JC dosed off repeatedly, but woke up just long enough to hear Reverend Liverpool say, "...Can two walk together, except they be agreed?"

"My mother says that!" JC said audibly with a big smile on his face. "He must've met my momma somewhere." Tina's mother looked at JC as if she was about to reply, but didn't.

After church was dismissed, Tina's mother grabbed JC's hand and squeezed it tightly.

"Every time I see you, I'm gone have you read a chapter out of the bible. You hear me."

"Yes, mamma," JC replied.

"...You're not taking my daughter to hell," she snapped.

Tina led her mother down the steps and signaled for JC to call her later. He smiled and nodded his head.

He spent that evening with his own mother. He told her everything that had happened and she laughed until she couldn't laugh anymore. However, she was glad that he went to church, even though she hadn't been herself. Mary was the type of person who regularly watched church on television, but rarely attended. Somewhere through the years she had left her Catholic roots and become protestant. JC had become the first person in our family to step inside a church since my death, twenty years prior to this day. I imagine the two of them slept well that night with the Rott's outside and JC in his old bedroom.

He hadn't slept in that bedroom in a long time, but his mother kept it tidy as if it were her very own so it was certain to be comfortable.

CHAPTER TEN

Deuce arrived at JC's just past noon Tuesday morning. JC was frying eggs and sausage when he knocked at the door.

"Come on, man," JC shouted.

"What's that I smell?" Deuce asked as he stepped in.

"Just a little somp'n I'm whipping up for breakfast."

"Yeah…" Deuce replied as he took a swig of his gin.

"…You up early. What's up?"

"It ain't nothing…Just had some stuff on my mind."

"Yeah? You want some of this? I can whip you up somp'n right quick."

"Man, I ain't no broad," Deuce jested, and they each laughed contemptuously.

"Yo! Check this… I need you to help me out today."

"Cool. What's up?"

"I need to go to Joes and get a car."

"Why you don't have him deliver it?"

"Cause I want you to help me…that alright with you?"

"Whatever, man. When we doing this?"

"...After I eat."

JC poured a cup of orange juice and grabbed his plate and walked into the living room and sat in the recliner by the television. Deuce kicked back on the couch and watched as JC tuned in to a talk show. There were two women on the show who were both supposedly pregnant by the same man. The guy, of course, denied that he was with either of them. Deuce grew increasingly impatient with the show and leaned back on the couch and pulled out a joint.

"You want some of this Jane?"

"Nah, I don't want none o' yo dirt weed. I got the real shit."

"...The real shit? Nigga, this is the real shit...that Tai weed."

"Gimme dat," JC said as he grabbed the joint and ran it under his nose. "A'ight! ...You moving this?"

"My personal stuff," Deuce exclaimed, "I sell them other niggas dirt weed, like dat shit you got." They both laughed and lit up together. After the second joint and the remaining gin, Deuce asked JC, "Who's ya fall guy?"

"What I need a fall guy for?"

"...For when things go wrong."

JC sat up in his recliner and took one last drag on the joint.

"Why you always asking stupid ass questions?" he answered. "This ain't corporate America, man. This ain't the motherfuckin White House and shit. This is South Oak Cliff: Blacks, Mexicans, and poor white folks. –They don't want one motherfucka's name when shit gets fucked up. They want a gang of motherfuckas, so you don't tell a po-po nothing. No matter what he thinks he knows, you act like you ain't never heard that shit in your life."

"That's the silliest shit I've ever heard," Deuce replied, "Niggas are out there snitching every day; giving each other up so they can go free..."

"People act on what they see and what they hear," JC interrupted. "If you control that, you control them."

"Man, you must be higher than me...over there philosophizing, talking some kind o' Plato-Socrates shit."

They laughed and then JC scratched his head and asked, "What happened to you the other night?" Deuce paused. He didn't know Mario called JC Saturday night when Antonio snatched him.

"Nothing man, some crack head threw a brick...threw a brick through my window and shit. I chased him 'round the block and was gonna beat his ass, but...uh, shit. I couldn't catch him."

"How was the pool game?" JC continued. "Pool game?"

"Yeah. You went to Johnnies to play pool, right?"

"Yeah. Yeah, but I was too pissed to play after the situation in the parking lot. I just had me a couple of drinks and something to eat."

"...So you were still hungry?"

"Yeah!"

"Who you have dinner with?"

Deuce hesitated and JC watched his demeanor as he replied, "...some broad. I don't remember her name. What's up with all these questions," Deuce retorted, "and what's up with this car we're picking up?"

"...Just making small talk. I noticed that bruise on your face and was just wondering. Anyway, it's Tina's car that we're picking up. I had the door fixed and I want to drop it off at her job tonight."

"What's up with this broad, man? You giving her tours and chunking her change. —You whipped?"

JC laughed at Deuces comment and grabbed the joint for one last toke.

"She's special," JC remarked. "...Don't know what it is yet, but she special."

"...a broad? Special?" Deuce replied, "Whateva man, let's get out of here."

The conversation wasn't much different from J.C's house to Mike's Garage, with Deuce growing increasingly annoyed with the special broad conversation.

"Man, these broads out to get what they can get," Deuce said, "The only difference between them is some are better at it than others."

"Well, what if there was a girl that gave you everything you needed," JC challenged. "Wouldn't you wanna do for her?"

"I don't need nothing from a broad, but some bed action," Deuce replied, and they each laughed and looked to the right as Deuce pulled into Mike's driveway.

"I'm wasting my time talking to you," JC continued. "We see things completely different. I don't need to hit everything that moves. I just want somebody in my corner that I can trip with every now and then."

"You wanna marry these broads...have babies and shit."

"Yeah, maybe."

"Please. —Get the hell out my car. I'm 'bout to go look at this Impala."

"That's what we're here for."

"What? ...This that broad's car?"

"Yeah."

"Tell me you didn't have all this done for her."

"It was the least I could do."

"Man, all I ever got a broad was a bed...and that was because the damn sleeper sofa kept folding up on us when we did it doggy-style."

Mike walked up as they were speaking. "I stripped it and rebuilt it from the ground up," he said. "...found out that it was an SS model, so I rebuilt it accordingly, with the Z03 options. The only thing I couldn't get hold of was the Impala SS horseshoe shifter and console, but it's really the same as those in a Chevy Chevelle, so that's what it has. Here's the key."

"You get the check?" JC asked.

"Yes, I did. Thank you. It wasn't about the money, but when I got the check I felt like all those all-nighters and the extra guy hired to build that 427 was worth it. It reminded me of when we put Betty together for you."

"Yeah. You're the man," JC said, smiling.

"Well, I hope ya'll enjoy it. You have any problems, give me a call."

"...Will do!" JC said as the two of them shook hands."

"You sure been generous lately, Deuce stated. "It's almost like you forgot that we owe Antonio $100,000."

"Antonio's been paid," JC announced.

"What? When did you pay him?"

"Same day Tony popped you in the shoulder. Why?"

Deuce paused. "You just never mentioned it," Deuce responded and then got into his car. He watched JC crank the Impala and drive off. He then lit a joint and took a toke. "What the hell's going on?" he said audibly.

That night around 8:45 JC arrived at Tina's job. He pulled a large red bow out of the trunk and fashioned it on the top of the car. He then waited at the entrance for her to come out. She was about 15 minutes longer than she should have been but JC waited patiently.

When she came out the door JC stood there with outstretched arms.

"Hey, baby! How was your day?"

"It was great!" she said excitedly. "I had my review and I got a raise!"

"Really? That's great…"

"What are you doing up here?" Tina asked.

"I came to see you."

"Oh yeah!"

"Yeah!"

"…You sure you ain't here to pick up that big booty girl you were staring at last time?"

"Girl, stop tripping. I came here to give you something."

"You proposing to me?"

"Hell no. —I mean, no, baby. I came to bring you your car. Tina looked at him contemptuously and then looked in the direction in which he was pointing.

"Where are you pointing?" she asked.

"Right here in front of you," he replied.

"What? That ain't my car!" she replied with an attitude, but once she noticed that JC was serious, her eyes began to water and two tears streamed down her cheek. "That's my car?"

"Yeah, baby that's your car."

She walked over to it and rubbed her hand gently across the Grotto blue paint and peeped through the window at the redone interior.

"Here's the key," JC said with a smile and almost instinctively she began to walk to the passenger's side of the car. She chuckles at her error and proceeds to the driver's door. She pressed the button and pulled at the door. It opened smooth and gently as if brand new. A few more tears fall as she sat in the seat and looked around. "Start it!" JC yelled. She lookup at him and turned the key. The Impala cranked right up and had a really smooth tone to it. Tina lowers her head to the steering wheel and began to cry. JC stood there a moment knowing that this had to be one of the happiest days of her life. Then suddenly she rushed out of the car and hugged him tightly. They stood there kissing for several minutes before she lets him go.

"Why'd you do that? I thought you were just getting the door fixed."

"I had the means to do it, so I did."

"I love you, Jonathan. Thank you. You're so sweet to me."

"You're welcome. ...Anything for my baby."

"You sure this car ain't for that big booty girl?" Tina asked.

JC smiled and then slapped her on the bottom. "Yeah, it's for my big booty girl." Tina then grabbed him and hugged him even tighter than before, snuggling her head firmly against his shoulder.

"Let's go to Xavier's and get something to eat," JC said as he lowered his head and kissed her neck.

"I can't," she replied, "I have to get my mother's prescription before the drug store closes.

"We can get the prescription and then get out and get something.

"I don't know JC. Why you always wanna go out so late. Why can't we go out earlier in the day?"

"...We can, but I wanna see you now as well. Come on. I'll follow you." Tina looked at him curiously and nodded yes.

"Here's your keys. Don't be slowing me down I told you I was in a hurry."

"Yes, ma'am," he replied, "Where'd you park the truck?"

"...Better find it if you plan to keep up," Tina said as she jumped into the car and pulled off.

"Oh! Okay!" JC yelled as he ran out to the parking lot

searching for his truck. He looked both right and left but did not see it. He then ran to the edge of the building and looked in the parking lot adjacent to it and there it was, parked at the far end of the parking lot. He ran to the truck as quickly as he could and was out of breath about time he climbed into it and cranked the engine. "Okay, now where would she go," he said audibly.

There were only two places that would likely be going to and both of them were in the Lake June area. JC sped towards the freeway, hoping to catch her before they reached Highway 35E but she obviously got used to her cars newfound power quicker than he'd thought. JC entered the ramp at Royal Avenue and immediately slowed when he saw her pulled over onto the shoulder. He pulled over and backed up to her car. He hurried out to see what was wrong.

"Tina!" he yelled as he approached the window. "What's wrong?"

"Nothing. I haven't had a car radio in a long time. I'm setting the presets."

"You're setting the presets on the side of the freeway?"

"Yea," she says with a big smile and then revs up the engine. "This baby moves. You better try and keep up. You know I'm in a hurry!"

Just as JC steps away, she peels the tires and powers up the highway at full throttle. JC assumes chase all the way to the neighborhood drug store on Mattison Street and Cooper Road. He pulls into the parking lot behind her and watched as she ran from the car to the doorway. She looked back at him and smiled when the door pushed open. These places are normally prompt at closing time; opening time, however, is another matter entirely.

He gets out of the truck and walked in after her. One of the store clerks were standing there with the keys about the time he came within reach of the door, but she still let him in. He walked up behind Tina staring at her luscious behind. He eagerly licked his lips as his fingers gently plodded up her hips to her waist. She sighed as he pulled her close and ran his lips gently across her neck and kissed her softly from her shoulder to her cheekbone. She pressed back against him surrendering herself to his calm caress. His hands wandered to her thigh on one side and her breast on the other. She shyly withdrew to avoid anyone noticing, but her low eyes told of her longings and her pouty lips trembled in anticipation. Her sensuality had been aroused and subtly exposed, and they each knew that the other wanted them. Tina's inner thigh began to tremble and she grabbed the hand that was moving down her thigh, but he pulled her in close and hugged her snuggly from behind. Again she sighed and watched her gentle protests go ignored.

Once the pharmacist approached with the prescription, she hurried to the counter and counted out the money to pay for it. He approached her slowly and grabbed her free hand after she had taken hold of the prescription. She gazed into his eyes and then quickly looked away. She could feel her body betraying her. Weakness set in her knees. As they exited the front door JC spun her around and lifted her chin to receive his kiss. Their lips gently touched. Their tongues avidly intertwined. She fought the heaviness that came over her body, the lust that set in her bones.

"I can't do this, JC," she said as she gazed into his eyes.

"...but I've wanted you from the first time I laid eyes on you."

They kissed again, his lips in hers and her lips in his. More tongue, more rubbing and touching, and caressing.

"I'd better get home," she said. And he replied, "I'll follow you."

She walked to her car and was constantly looking back at JC. She unlocked the passenger's door and got inside. After climbing over to the driver seat and putting the key in the ignition, she shook her head in embarrassment. She had, just that quickly, forgotten that her car door had been fixed.

Tina's house was only a couple of blocks down Cooper Road so the ride there was fairly quick. JC hopped out the truck and walked towards the porch to intercept her. He grabbed her hand as she reached for the door and took both of them in his. Their lips found refuge in each other once again. She pants as his lips kiss and nibble at her neck and his hands find their way below her skirt and up her thighs to the roundness of her bottom. He clenched her cheeks tightly in each hand as his tongue made its way back into her mouth. She leaned forward giving in totally to his advances. Her body went limp, as he grew stiff. Her head laid gently on his shoulder as his fingers wandered to her panty line and then underneath. He caressed the roundness of her behind and slowly brought a hand forward over the crown of her hips and down to the freshly manicured hairs of her vulva. The wind was soft and steady and the end of her skirt slightly flapped in the breeze. She could feel her flesh wax warm against him. Her juices had wet her panties and JC was well aware. His middle finger brushed lightly across her opening as his left hand cupped her treasure. Just then, they heard a shuffling from the house as her mother approached the door. JC backed away from Tina and was staring deep into her eyes as the door opened.

"Baby, why you standing out here so long? —Oh, Jonathan," her mother said in an indifferent tone.

"Hey Momma," JC replied.

"Boy, why you call me momma. I ain'tcha momma. Hell, I

don't wantcha trying to get all close to me. Girl, getcha ass in here. It's late."

"Okay Momma," Tina replied, "I'll be right in."

"A'ight now, don't be long. I'm ready to take my medicine and go to sleep."

Tina's mother walked away but she left the door wide open so she could listen. JC looked through the screen to see if she had gone into another room. "I'm right here. Don't thank I ain't seen'cha looking at my daughter with them Calderon eyes. Hurry up and get yo ass off my porch."

"Bye Jonathan," Tina said as she lowered her head.

"I'll see you soon," he replied.

Tina looked up at him and smiled, then opened the screen door and walked in. JC stood there watching as she gently closed and locked the door. "Getcho ass off my porch!" her mother yelled, and JC did just that.

Tina's mother didn't say much to her she just looked at her rather intently as she opened the bag and pulled out the prescription and handed it to her mother. Tina then walked into the kitchen and grabbed a glass from the cupboard, rinsed it out and began to tell her mother about her day. Her mother was mostly silent throughout the conversation. When she took the glass from Tina, she took notice of the bunching of her clothes in the back but said nothing about it.

After their short visit with each other, Tina went to her room and turned on the radio and lit a candle. Her spirit still aroused from her night with JC, she turned off the light and stood before the mirror removing her clothes and once she was down to nothing but her panties, she slowly moved over to the bed and laid back in it. The mood was just right for a romantic voyage into intimacy. The room was just dark enough to hide her details but not her silhouette from any would be watchers at the window. The candle burning before the mirror created the kind of ambiance that you would expect to see in an erotic bathhouse. The radio station had played a series of slow ballads before entering into the slow mix session of its programming. Several minutes later, her mother walked up to her door and leaned forward to listen, but the music was all she heard so she moseyed on to her room.

Tina's eye closed as a Luther Vandross song came on. Her hands cupped her breasts tenderly and moved ever so gently across her nipples. She squeezed them tightly as she rolled over onto her back. Her mouth opened wide as her head rolled back and a faint moan came out. Her hands rubbed her voluptuous breasts from side to side and her legs opened wide. The movements gradually quickened as the intensity grew. One hand ventured down to her panties and skimped across the wetness at its center, rubbing it as if it were fine Egyptian cotton tickling the tiny sensors above and below her fingertips. This went on for several minutes before her movements came to a gratifying end. She slept the rest of the night through, peacefully and still.

CHAPTER ELEVEN

The following morning Tina was up bright and early. She washed up and fixed her hair up nicely with lots of flowing curls. She also spent a few moments longer than normal applying makeup and ensuring that her ensemble was flawless. Her mother could hear her singing with the music blasting from her room so she went to investigate. Tina was dancing in the middle of the room with her hairbrush held firmly in her hands like it was a microphone.

"What's wrong, baby," her mother asked.

"Fiiiiiiiya," Tina sang loudly.

"Her mother slammed the door shut and walked back to the kitchen. Tina came out fifteen minutes later and grabbed the phone off the kitchen wall and called up Sheila and told her to get dressed up real pretty because she was coming through to pick her up. Tina's mother stood next to the table with her hands on her hips staring at her. Tina quickly hung up with Sheila and called Daphne.

"Girl, get dressed! I'll be there to get you in an hour. If you ain't as pretty as me, then that's too bad for you."

"What's going on?" Daphne asked.

"We're going to lunch!"

"Lunch?"

"Yeah, girl ...be there in an hour," Tina yelled as she hung up the phone and danced over to her mother singing.

"What the hell's going on with you," her mother asked.

"I'm alive!" she yelled as she grabbed her mother's hands and spun her around with her. Her mother jerked her hands away.

"You done lost yo damn mind, girl. What's wrong with you?"

"Nothing, Ma... can't I just be happy?"

"You be yo ass happy in a chair."

"Ah, Ma."

"I ain't playing with you, lil girl. Sit down." Tina grabbed a chair and sat down and her mother did the same. "This 'bout that lil nappy headed boy?"

"Well, kinda."

"Kinda?" Her mother said as she looked at Tina out of the corner of her eyes. "You having sex?"

"No, Momma!" Tina laughed. "I'm saving that for the one."

"The one?"

"Yea Momma!" Tina laughed more dearly, "We had this conversation before. ...The one I marry, Ma."

"Okay," Tina's mother continued, "Afterwards!" "Huh?"

"...After he marries you. You give him some after he marries you. Hell! ...A man ain't gone buy the cow if he can get the milk for free." Tina laughed and then got up and hugged her mother.

"I love you, Momma. Be sure you take your medicine."

"Don't worry 'bout me. You be careful, and I love you too."

Tina got into her '68 Impala and burned out of the driveway in a fashion more common to Treasure than herself. She got to Gardenview Drive and Worldstore Court in a matter of minutes and honked her horn repeatedly for Sheila to come out. The neighbors were out on the porch watching her bob her head and sing to the blasting music. Not many people had stereo systems that played both loudly and clearly so it drew a little attention from the neighbors. Sheila ran outside.

"Oh my god, is this your car?" She yelled.

"I can't hear you," Tina Replied.

"I said is this your car!"

"Girl, you know I can't hear you over the jams!" Tina jumped out of the car and hugged her friend. "Girl, ain't it pretty?"

"Yeah. I thought he was just fixing your door."

"I did too but, he hooked me up, girl. Get in! Let's go get Daphne."

A half-hour later they were pulling up to Daphne's house. Tina turned down her music as she entered the driveway. The guys hanging out on the corner were looking at the car with envy. "Hey!" one of them yelled, "Whose car you driving?" Tina and Sheila didn't reply they just chuckled as they exited the car and greeted Daphne who was coming out of the house as they arrived.

"Girl, whose car is this?" Daphne yelled.

"It's mine."

"Don't tell me that boy did this to your car."

"Then I won't tell ya," Tina replied, "Come on. Let's go."

"Tina," Daphne shouted as she grabbed her arm. "Tell me that boy didn't do this to your car, girl."

"He did it and I like it," Tina replied. "Now, if you're coming, come on."

They all got into the car and pulled away. The guys on the corner tried to stop them, but they kept on going. After a few minutes, Daphne eased up and sung along with Tina, Sheila and the music. They were drawing attention the whole way up Stanton Boulevard to Lake June.

"Where do y'all want to eat?" Tina asked.

"I want something different," Sheila suggested with a big smile.

"I'm not too crazy about what we eat," Daphne added, "I just want to hurry up and get something."

"I heard 'bout this Jamaican place off Embassy Street," Sheila added. "Y'all wanna go there?"

"Sounds alright to me," Tina replied.

"Alright," Daphne added, "I'ma get me some Jerk Chicken."

"Jamaican place, here we come," Tina yelled.

About ten minutes later they arrived at Caribbean Nites Bar & Grill. They laughed at the yellow painted brick and high grass as they parked. It was officially lunch hour all over Dallas as people rushed in and out trying to get a decent bite to eat before having to go back to work. As Tina and her girls approached the door Kevin, the long-haired Jamaican, greeted them.

"Hey, Mon...table fa tree?"

"Yeah, table fa tree," Sheila answered. Everyone laughed at her wannabe Jamaican accent. Kevin sat them at a table near the bar and another woman came out to their table and took their order. They looked about the dimly lit room at the banners of the Jamaican flag, a roaring lion and the beloved Bob Marley on the nearby yellow and green painted walls. They loved the welcoming atmosphere and began to really get into the theme. Within minutes, Kevin came back to their table.

"Ya won beer, Pretty ladies?"

"No, we're not even old enough to drink," Daphne replied.

"Dis Yaad, here, Mon," Kevin replied. "If yah con wok, ya con drink."

"Okay," Tina interjects proudly, overriding Daphne. "Give me something nice."

"Okay...and you ladies?" Kevin asked Sheila and Daphne.

"Give me whatever you give her," Sheila answers.

"Hey, you're underage...both of you!" Daphne yelled. Then she looked at Kevin and said mockingly, "I don won no likka mon."

"Den we get wattah for you, Miss pretty," Kevin answered. Everyone was laughing at Daphne. She was always the uptight one. Her family was real religious and she thought everything was a sin. This did not hamper the spirits of the other two who walked over to the pool tables and picked up the sticks.

"Let's play a game until our food is ready," Tina said.

"Okay," Sheila said as she rolled the balls out onto the table, "You know how to play?

"No!" Tina cried out, "Do you?"

"No."

"Then perhaps I'll show you," said a voice in the darkness. As he drew closer, Tina could see that it was Deuce. She froze in her steps, petrified from head to toe. Deuce came up behind Sheila, placed his hand in the small of her back and bent her over to the table with his other hand. He leaned over her body so that they touched as he showed her how to line the stick up with the ball. Sheila looked at his arms guiding the stick in her hands. "You want to line up with your target. Your stroke should be smooth and strong, never weak. Even when you shoot softly, you want your stroke to be solid and deliberate," Deuce whispers as they hit the ball and it fell in the corner pocket. He stood up and slapped Sheila on the bottom. "Lesson over." She flushed as he stepped away. Tina was still frozen in place when he approached her.

"I know you, don't I?"

"Yes, Tina said as she trembled at his sight. He cupped her face in his hand and looked into her eyes.

"Did we fuck?"

"No!" Tina shouted as she stepped back and looked over at Sheila.

"Okay," Deuce continued, "We'll have to do something 'bout that. Perhaps I can do you and your friend together."

Tina slowly backed away and then ran to her table. Sheila followed her and Deuce went on about his business. Their food and drinks were already there at the table when they sat down.

"Who's that?" Sheila asked as she adjusted her seat, "That brotha's fine.

"That brotha's a gangsta!" Tina shouted.

"So what, you're dating a gangsta,"

"...and you need to stop," Daphne added.

"Why?" Tina asked, "Because he's the first man to ever really give a darn about me? Please! ...and he's not a gangsta. He just has gangsta friends like that ass over there."

"...so you do know him?" Sheila asked.

"I've met him. He's a liar, a cheat, and a womanizer. My boyfriend doesn't even trust him."

"...Your boyfriend?" Daphne retorted. "He's your boyfriend after what...a week and a half?"

"Yes," Tina exclaimed modestly.

"Did I miss something?" Daphne continued, "You are not yourself Tina. You need to slow down."

"What are you talking about?"

"I'm talking about— you just broke up with Ronald and you know you still love him," Daphne explained.

"I never loved him," Tina replied, "He was a pig! Why are we even talking about this?"

"…Because your tripping," Daphne continued. "I have seen you get dogged out too many times and you think this slick talking gangsta from Lake June is going to be any different?"

"How you know he's a Lake June gangsta, huh?" Tina yelled, "How come he can't be a businessman with a really good job?"

"…Because he ain't!" Daphne and Sheila replied, nearly simultaneously.

"How ya'll know?"

"How much you think it cost to get your car done like he did it?" Daphne asked.

"…And in a week," Sheila added.

"Oh, you're on her side now?" Tina asked as she turned to Sheila.

"No," Sheila lied, "I'm not on anybody's side, but you need to stop tripping. You know that man's a Lake June gangsta. Nobody has cash like that in P.G. but Lake June gangstas."

"What about that girl Lynnette," Tina interjected, "her people got money and it's from running a business."

"…On Lake June!" they said, almost in unison.

"So dem dar some ganstas too, Sheila said in her Jamaican accent. They all laughed at her silliness and ordered another round of drinks. This time Daphne had one too. Before all was said and done, Daphne had about three rounds of Long Island Ice Teas.

"Are you alright, girl," Sheila asked as she looked over at Daphne rocking in her chair.

"Yeah, I feel good, girl. What's in them iced teas?" "I don't know but they off the chain ain't they?"

"Yeah girl, I almost want to go out there and dance."

They all laughed at her, swaying back and forth, eyes half-open, now trying to dance in her chair."

"Come on girl!" Sheila said to Daphne, "Let's go dance." They laughed and joked together as they headed to the dance floor. Tina remained in her chair and cheered them on from there. Sheila and Daphne danced two songs before Sheila came back to her chair, leaving Daphne to solo the next two songs alone before she wobbled back to her seat. They all laughed and joked about her condition and how they had never seen her have so much fun. Tina and Daphne then went to the restroom. Sheila had one last drink before she reached her limit, but it wasn't long before Deuce approached her again.

"What's up lady?" he asked.

"Nothing," Sheila said dejectedly.

"Where're your girls?"

"They went to the restroom. They'll be back in a minute."

"Is that right?"

"That's right," Sheila replied nervously as he had a seat in front of her, "...and that's my girl's chair you're sitting in."

"...So. She can sit on my lap," Deuce replied. "What's your name?"

"Tiffany."

"Hmm, you don't look like a Tiffany. You wouldn't be lying to me would you?"

"Why does it matter? It ain't like we're gonna hook up or nothing." Deuce smiled and reached over and touched her thigh. She jerked away and looked at him sternly.

"You didn't say stop," he said, "In fact, I can hear your pussy calling me."

"My pussy don't know your name, man," Sheila said and jumped up from her chair and rushed to the restroom to find Tina and Daphne. They were exiting just as she approached.

"What's wrong," Tina asked.

"He was talking to my pussy, girl."

"What?" Tina laughed.

"Let's get the hell out o' here." Tina and Daphne laughed at her behavior and proceeded to the register to pay their tab. There was another person ahead of them so they laughed and joked among themselves as they waited. Deuce walked past them and handed the person at the register a hundred dollar bill. "This should cover their tab and the tip." Tina paused as he approached her. "I do know you," he said. "You see, I went outside for a moment to smoke on a lil something and noticed your car. Ha! --It's nice being JC's bitch ain't it." They were all silent as he circled around her like a vulture circles road kill. "Well, now that you're marked I guess the rest of us will just have to imagine how sweet that pussy is, huh?" As he stopped, he looked over at Sheila, smiled and walked off.

As they walked out, everyone outside paused and watched them get into the car. It was silent as they drove off, but as soon as they turned the corner, everyone started talking at the same time.

"Who was that?" Daphne asked.

"What does he mean 'bout you being marked?" Sheila asked.

Tina stared straight ahead shaking like a leaf. A lone tear fell and ran down her cheek. Her mouth opened as if she was about to say something but nothing came out. She looked at Sheila and another tear fell. She immediately pulled over onto the side of the road and walked to the back of the car and threw up. Sheila and Daphne exited after her. Tina leaned back against the car crying. Daphne grabbed her purse and pulled out some napkins.

"What's wrong, girl?" Daphne asked.

"I just need to get some fresh air," Tina replied.

"Well, let's get off this road," Sheila said. "Here, I'll drive. You just get in."

Sheila then drives down Lake June towards the Lake June Roundabout, which was really more like a large traffic circle because the central island was open to the public and is the site of the yearly Fourth of July fireworks show. The center of the roundabout is 200 yards across and outfitted like a small park. They pulled over at David Banner's Night Club and walked across the street to the park. They sat at a table and started to talk. Tina told them how she knew Deuce and why she was so struck with fear when she saw him. As they were speaking, a woman walked up to them and asked them if they wanted to order anything. They all laughed.

"What you mean? What are you selling," Sheila asked.

"I serve meals and drinks from the surrounding restaurants. As you can see there are five restaurants on the Lake June Roundabout and they all serve the patrons of the park at no extra cost."

"So, I can just come to the park and have a seat and someone will come over here and serve me?"

"Well, if you look on the side of the table where you leg is there's a button you push that pages us."

"Oh, so I'm hitting the button?" Daphne asked.

"Yes," the woman pleasantly replied.

"Oh, I'm sorry," Daphne remarked as they all took note of the button her leg had been pressing against, "but we've already eaten."

"Alright."

"Well, I am still hungry," Tina said, "What choices do we have?"

The server then thumbed through the menus with them until

they settled for an appetizer tray from Alimento Del Cielo, an upscale Mexican Restaurant right across from them. The food was prepared and served rather quickly, and they each picked from the tray and sipped on lemonade as they talked. After some time passed, they pressed the button again for the server. This time a gentleman came out to them.

"I want to take care of our tab," Tina stated.

"I apologize, Mrs. Sanchez, your tab has been cleared."

"What?" Sheila yelled.

"How do you know my name?" Tina asked, but the gentleman simply smiled, lowered his head and wished them a safe and prosperous evening.

"What you doing, girl?" Sheila asked, "Why are we getting stuff for free today?"

"I don't know," Tina replied.

"I know," Daphne said in a half-slurred voice, "It's that boy you dating. Didn't the dude at the club say you were marked? That's what he was talking 'bout."

"Can't be," Tina replied.

"Baby, this is Lake June. I wouldn't be surprised if you never paid for anything else 'round here," Sheila added.

"Girl, stop tripping," Tina replied as she got up from her seat.

"Well, let's go walk around," Sheila suggested. "You always wanted to walk Lake June and we're all off today...and—it's daytime, so it's not too busy."

"She's got a point," Daphne added.

"Shut up. You're drunk." Tina said mockingly. "Both of you heifers are drunk."

"You ain't walking too straight yourself, Mrs. Sanchez," Sheila retorted.

They then walked west down Lake June, noting all the shops

that they previously had only seen while driving past in a car. They looked at shoes, tried on clothes and window shopped for more than an hour. Then Tina pointed out the restaurant where she and JC first connected. They were particularly interested in the story about Xavier's Tropical Jubilee and asked her to tell them about it again. They each were hanging on every word as if she had never told them before. JC was, to them, like a great storybook character that appeared out of thin air. He was too good to be true. They never eased up on the questions and constantly begged for details, but Tina only shared enough to wet their appetites.

After long, Daphne had sobered up a bit and was back to her old uptight self, questioning JC's motives and accusing Tina of falling for him too soon. However, Tina rejected all of her negative comments and grew increasingly tired of the accusations.

"Why you all in my business anyway?" Tina shouted.

"I'm just looking out for you," Daphne replied.

"You're getting on my nerves with that nagging."

"I'm not nagging. You know that guy's up to no good and you know ya'll are going too fast. Next week you'll be telling us you're pregnant."

"Hello! I'm not that easy. You must've forgotten who you were talking to."

"What do you mean by that?" Sheila interjected. "You trying to break on me on the sly?"

"No, girl," Tina said, "but if the shoe fits…"

"What!" Sheila screamed and the two of them burst into laughter. "Well, hell, if it itches scratch it." Sheila added, "…but you know what? That guy at the Jamaican place was hot as hell. He spoke to my pussy, girl." Tina and Daphne laughed hysterically when she said that. "For real," Sheila continued, "He said, I can hear your pussy calling me, and sho'nuff, my pussy got so wet it embarrassed the hell out of me." Tina laughed so hard that tears began to fall. "I hope he didn't know he affected me like that." Sheila continued. "That was so embarrassing."

"That's nasty!" Daphne alleged.

"Girl," Sheila said, "you wait until you get you some. You won't be talking 'bout nastiness like its nasty no more." Then she looked at Tina who was still trying to get herself together. "I'm talking to you, too."

"What?" Tina asked.

"You had any?"

"I ain't telling you that!"

"That's because you're a lil' virgin, too."

"...and what's wrong with that?"

"Nothing...just don't know what you're missing."

"Yes I do," Tina murmured.

"What you say?" Sheila shouted. "That boy put that thang on you already?"

"No. Well, almost." Tina replied.

"Well, tell us!" Sheila shouted.

"There's nothing to tell you. We just got close."

"How'd it feel?" Sheila asked.

"You know how it felt. ...And Daphne, don't you say nothing. I already know what you're gonna say. 'Y'all going too fast!' -- And so what? I like it."

"Mmmm, Momma 'bout to get her some," Sheila declared.

"No. I just like him a lot."

"Okay. Okay. I feel you. ...So you think you can work me something with his friend?"

"Hell no, Tina retorted, "He's a pig! Why you want him?"

"Just asking..." Sheila replied.

"Y'all too fast for me," Daphne said while shaking her head in disapproval."

"Hey! Let's go to Xavier's." Tina shouted.

"We can't go in there," Daphne replied. "That place's expensive. ...look at it."

"Don't worry about it. I just want to say hi to a friend."

They walked in the foyer and asked the hostess if they could speak to Xavier. She sat them at a table next to the door and told them that she would go and check. Sheila and Daphne scanned the room taking special note of its extravagance. Sheila complained that the music was making her sleepy but Daphne seemed to like it a lot. They were there about twenty minutes before Xavier came out. However, when he did, he had with him a large silver tray with three deserts atop. The girls all marveled as he personally served each of them a succulent slice of fudge covered chocolate cake topped with whip cream and a lone strawberry.

"So, what brings you to Lake June, Ms. Tina?" he said.

"I was just hanging out with my girls and stopped by to say hello."

"Okay, and who are these lovely ladies?

"Well, this is Sheila, I've known her since I was eight and this is Daphne. She goes to my church, and I've known her for about three years now."

"Alright. Well, I am pleased to have met you, beautiful ladies. I hope to see you again sometime."

"You will," Daphne replied.

Xavier nodded and then excused himself. Tina and Sheila then ragged on Daphne about her response to Xavier, but she maintained that she was just being polite. They walked back to the car after they had finished their dessert. More time had passed than they had thought. It was almost six o'clock and the sun had already begun to fall. The sky was a Crimson red and a cool breeze had come through.

When they got back to David Banner's, there was a guy outside passing out flyers. They each took one and got into the car. Sheila read the flyer out loud, "Wednesday Night Live, come and hear your favorite comedians perform like never before. – Doors open at 8 PM, $2 well drinks, and ladies get in for free until 10 PM."

"Y'all wanna go?" Tina asked.

"I don't, Daphne replied, "I'm not feeling too good."

"I do," Sheila answered, "but we need to go get in some better clothes."

"Yeah, because we've gots to be fly," Tina declared.

"Look at you," Sheila ranted, "you're sho'nuff perky today."

Tina looked at her and smiled while bobbing her head to the music. They both laughed and continued on with their conversation. They dropped Daphne off at home first so that Tina and Sheila, who lived around the corner from each other, were not rushed. Tina took about an hour and a half to get dressed and another 30 minutes or so talking to her mother.

When she finally arrived at Sheila's house, Sheila still wasn't dressed so they talked and joked around as she finished up. Once they were done, they were as striking as two movie stars, flawless from head to toe. They arrived at the club at about 9:40 and drew the attention of every man they passed. Once they got through the line and to the door, the security person asked them for their IDs. He looked at them closely then looked back at the girls.

"I'm sorry ladies," he advised, "You have to be 21 to enter."

"Come on, man," Sheila followed, "We didn't get all dressed up for nothing?"

"I'm sorry," he repeated, "You sure look like grownups to me, but if the cops come up in here, we'll have hell to pay."

"It's ok," Tina replied.

"Girl, I didn't get all dressed up for nothing," Sheila snapped. "I've been wanting to come up here forever. Ain't there something you can do? Tell them who your man is."

"I'm sorry ladies…" the security person butted in, "but you have to go now.

"Hey!" Sheila shouted, "Do you know Deuce?"

"Deuce?" he snapped.

"Yeah," Sheila replied, "That's my man and he is expecting me to meet him up in there in a half hour."

He started laughing and then rubbed his chin curiously. One of the other security guards yelled over for him to come and give them a hand with the searches, but he held up his hand as if he was telling him to hold on. His lips firmed around the edges as he looked back at the girls. "You should be careful –the names you throw around," he said, "Deuce is not the type who keeps a woman and he is definitely not the type that would show up or be welcomed here. Now, I don't know how you know him, but I would suggest you stay away from him."

"Man, you gone let us in?" Sheila groaned.

"No. –Now… run along now, lil' bunnies, before the wolves get 'hold of you."

Tina grabbed Sheila's hand and pulled her away.

"Forget it, girl," she said, "I know where we can go."

"Where?" Sheila said with attitude.

"Crimson Moon!"

"We're going to have the same problem there," Sheila said.

"No, we won't. I can get us in."

"How?"

"Just come on. You'll see." They got back into the car and drove down Lake June towards Crimson Moon. It was only 10:30 and the streets were already stirring with characters of various sorts. They were only about two blocks down the road before Sheila suggested that they just get out and walk. Tina gladly obliged and pulled over at Fat Daddy's Smoke Pit. The tantalizing aroma it gave off could be smelt a block away. Fat Daddy's had a large outside seating area, as did most of the Lake June restaurants, which was surrounded by an old ranch-style fence. Tina and Sheila glanced over at all of the patrons who sat out there chomping down on what some say is the best barbecue in Dallas. Xavier's parking lot could be seen across the street. It was full and had parking attendants scattered about directing cars.

"Damn girl, what your friend got going on over there?" Sheila asked.

"That place's always packed. They be having a live band up in there and everything."

"For real? I bet they be playing some ol' corny stuff from the "50's."

"Naw, girl, they be playing some nice songs up in there."

"Yeah," Sheila said, "Whatever. ...Like that sleepy stuff they were playing earlier."

Tina laughed at her friend. Sheila was new-school, not at all interested in the classics. She was sold on Funk, Pop and anything else she could dance to.

The two of them were only four blocks from Crimson Moon, but four blocks of Lake June offers more than the local mall in some cities. Hence, the reason they window-shopped every apparel store along the way until they were distracted by voices coming from between two of the buildings. There was a rhythmic tapping of toms and rapping of buckets and cans accompanying those alluring voices and sounded very unique and somehow tribal.

They stepped into the alley and peeked around the corner of the building where they saw around 35 to 40 people standing around a 50-gallon drum of burning wood reciting poetry. A makeshift band stood among them beating on anything that would make a sound. They listened to three different people recite their poetry before someone noticed them and motioned for them to come over. They wanted to hear more but were afraid and ran from the alley to the street laughing all the while.

Once they reached Crimson Moon. They walked up to the door and pulled the security person aside.

"I know we are supposed to be 21 to get in," Tina said, "but my boyfriend is the manager here and he said it would be ok for us to come by."

"Alright, let me get him," the security person replied.

A few moments later, Greg showed up at the door.

"How can I help you ladies?" he said while focusing his eyes on Sheila.

"Who are you?" Tina asked.

"I'm Greg Shepps, the manager. I was told that you asked for me."

"I was looking for Jonathan," Tina snapped.

"I'm sorry, I don't know that name."

"JC!" Tina shouted. "You know JC don't you?"

"I'm sorry, ma'am."

"This is crazy," Tina shouted. "What about Sync? I guess you don't know Sync either?"

"I'm sorry ma'am," Greg said with a shrewd look on his face,

"Perhaps I can allow you to use the phone and make a call."

"I don't wanna make no damn call!" Tina shouted, but Sheila gently took Tina by the hand and whispered in her ear.

"Girl, I think you should go ahead and make that call." Tina looked at her half-confused.

"What?"

"Let's go call your man," Sheila said with a devilish grin on her face.

"Okay," Tina said while looking sideways at Sheila.

"Okay then, follow me," Greg said as he lifted the velvet rope and allowed them in. Just as they passed the concession stand to the right of the entrance, Tina nudged Greg.

"Hey! I thought Jonathan was the manager here."

Greg laughed. "I'm sorry but I'm the manager here, Ms. Sanchez."

Tina and Sheila looked at each other in awe.

"How do you know my name?" Tina asked.

"Like I said, I'm the manager here," Greg replied. "It's my job to know things. —I'm actually glad you showed up tonight. I can go ahead and get you set up."

"Set up with what?" Sheila asked.

"I'll get you too, Ms. Wilson." "Oh hell nawl," Tina shouted, "somebody's gonna tell me how you know our whole damn name.

"Just follow me back to the office, please."

Tina stopped Sheila and was about to turn around when Greg came back to them and placed a hand on each of their shoulders. "Hey, I just need to take your pictures to finish your IDs."

"What IDs?" Tina asked.

"The IDs that will allow you to get around without

restrictions."

"Fake IDs?" Sheila retorted. "Are you talking 'bout hooking a sister up with some fake IDs?"

"They're enhanced Identification devices that even the department of public safety can't distinguish from your actual issue."

"How do you do this?" Tina asked.

"I'm sorry ma'am," Greg replied, "I'm sure you will ask your man that, given the opportunity. Now come along while you can."

They followed Greg into a small room across from JC's office. Their pictures were taken and in a matter of minutes, and their new IDs were issued. Tina's ID stated that she was 21 and Sheila's stated that she was 22.

"Keep these IDs separate. When you carry these, leave your real ones at home and when you carry the real ones leave these at home so that you're never caught with both of them on you," Greg suggested. They each agreed and then Greg added, "This should help you guys out of a lot of trouble and keep you from tossing around names like "JC", Ms. Sanchez, or "Deuce", Ms. Wilson. ...Unless, of course, that's what you want."

"How do you know 'bout that?" Sheila asked.

"Big Shepps is my brother," Greg replied. "The guy you spoke with at David Banner's, he called me as soon as he sent you off, so I called the boss and asked him what he wanted me to do and he said to hook you up with some ID's."

"What do you mean, the boss?" Tina asked. "Who is that?"

"...Must you ask," Greg replied? "JC. He owns the place. ...has from the beginning."

"What?" Tina shouted. "Why you playing with me?"

"I'm sorry Ms. Sanchez," Greg chuckled, "I thought you knew.

Any case, I have some things to tend to so you girls go out there and have some fun."

"Ok," Tina agreed happily.

"...You better come back and dance with me, too..." Sheila said under her voice as Greg walked away.

"I will," he answered as he glanced back at her. Tina and Sheila laughed and then walked back into the club. There was a standup comic on the stage and everyone seemed to be lounging around enjoying him so Tina and Sheila found an empty table so that they may do the same.

"Girl! This is what I'm talking 'bout," Sheila shouted. "Got you an entre-pre-negga."

"Girl, you're so corny..." Tina told her. "Jonathan doesn't own this club. He probably just had that guy lie for him to try and impress me."

"Girl, are you high?" Sheila shouted. "He ain't got to impress you with the words of some other brotha. Hell, he fixed your car up better than Chevrolet did...and from what I see, he has you connected with some real-life Lake June Gangstas. Getting you free food, fake IDs and a break from them lame wanna-be thugs we went to school with. —If you ask me, you're just in denial. ...and JC's fine! What's really going on?"

Tina didn't reply. She just looked up at the stage, somewhere beyond the comic and beyond the moment. It was silent at their table until the comedian finished his act. They had a few drinks here and there and listened to the music.

After a short while, a nice slow R&B song came on and Greg approached the table and asked Sheila to dance. Sheila gently grasped his hand and slowly rose from her seat. He stepped to her and cupped the smallness of her waist and slowly passed his hand along her body to the small of her back. Her face flushed as he looked deep into her eyes and stepped closer so that their bodies touched. They danced endlessly like long lost lovers reunited and you could see the passion grow hotter and hotter between them. She had become like putty in his hands. His every move flowed with hers and her every move flowed right along with his. Sheila's head fell lax against his neck as his hands clenched her bottom and they began a slow steady grind. The floor was pretty much empty after two songs but the DJ gladly obliged their lust-filled dance by rolling right into the next love song.

Tina watched the passion grow nearly out of control before she hurried from her seat to Sheila's rescue. She grabbed Sheila's arm and asked her if she was okay. Sheila pulled away and threw her arms snuggly around Greg's waist and continued her grind.

"Girl, if you don't get your hot ass off this floor. I'ma call your momma down here to get you."

"What's wrong with you?" Sheila replied, "We're just dancing."

"Girl, people are watching you get your groove on. Will you come on?"

Just then Greg gently kissed Sheila on the forehead and reached into his pocket for his business cards.

"I would like to keep in touch," he said, "Call me if you feel the same."

She took the business card and walked away with Tina, steadily glancing back at Greg who stood there like someone who had just been robbed of all his earthly goods.

After they had left the club, Tina asked Sheila about the dance.

"What were you doing getting your freak on in front of all

them folks?"

"Girl, I was just dancing," Sheila replied.

"Dancing? Everybody else was dancing. You were screwing."

"Oh! You're jealous?"

"No! –I have a man."

"Well, maybe I do too." Tina stopped and looked at her curiously.

"Oooo, girl, there's something you ain't told me ain't it?"

"Well," Sheila said shyly, "remember when I spent the summer with my aunt in Houston two years ago?"

"Yeah."

"Well, that was the guy I lost my virginity to."

"Greg?"

"Yeah girl, I knew it looked like him when he came to the door, but I wasn't sure. I mean right here in Dallas? ...I used to try and find him every time I went back to my aunts, but no one ever knew where he was. He just vanished...and it ain't like he could've gone over to my aunt's house and ask 'bout me."

"Girl, that man's like four or five years older than you."

"I know."

"...Look at you," Tina said, "you're soft on him already."

"...No softer than you are on Jonathan and I think I have more reason to be."

"Why?"

"...'Cause we have a history. –Greg and I have chemistry."

"Girl, please," Tina replied. "A couple o' hours ago your pussy was talking to another man."

They then burst out in laughter and threw their arms around each other, sharing a sisterly hug. A few bystanders whistled and raved but the two of them merely laughed and started back for the car. They laughed and joked a lot along the way but maintained a brisk walk because it was late.

Once they were securely in the car. They each let out a sigh of relief followed by a big smile.

"Girl, I had so much fun," Sheila said.

"Me too," Tina seconded.

"This was like the best Wednesday ever."

"I know, and where did the time go?"

"Oooo girl, it's almost 2 a.m. My dad's gonna have a cow.

"Yeah, that man's the only person I know crazier than you."

As Tina pulled out of the driveway, they looked up the road ahead of them. Lake June was lit up for as far as you could see, and though few places were still open, it still looked like they were.

CHAPTER TWELVE

O nce Friday came around Deuce and Mario were poised to make the money Antonio had requested. They met at Deuce's house around 6 a.m. to go over the plans for an armored truck heist they were planning to carry out that afternoon. Mario had brought along the two additional men Deuce requested and, once they were all in the house, Deuce closed and locked the door behind them. They all sat at the kitchen table and went over the details.

"Now this is very important," Deuce said, "Once the carrier comes out of the store, you wait until he begins to reach for the door of the truck because the driver won't unlock the door until the last minute. That'll give me time to get up and jump into the truck."

"Why don't we just grab the bag in his hand?" one of the men asked.

"...Because we have no way of knowing how much is in the bag or if anything's in the bag," Deuce replied. "We have to take the truck. –Once I make the block, I'm jumping right on I635 and then exiting Luna road. It all goes down at the hotel there. We'll have 'bout 10 minutes to get the can open and be gone so y'all be ready. –A'ight?"

"Yeah," the man replied while wiping the sweat from his brow.

"...Sounds like you done this before, Deuce," Mario remarked.

"I've done a lot of things. You ready?"

"Yeah, dude. All I have to do is drive the getaway car, but what's ol' buddy here gone do?"

"He's gone ride with you and once he sees the truck at the hotel he's gonna get out and help me unload it."

Just then Deuce sat up in his seat to light a cigarette and noticed his front door open. He got up and walked to the door and looked outside but no one was out there and nothing looked unusual, so he closed the door and walked back inside. "Didn't I lock that damn door?"

"I thought you did," Mario replied, "but hell, I don't know for sho' my mind was on this money."

Just after three o'clock the armored truck pulled up to the Stop and Shop off Marsh Road and I635. The carrier jumped out of the truck smiling and nodding his head to a kid that walked by with his mother. A few seconds later a parcel truck pulled alongside the armored truck and Deuce exited unnoticed from a trap door beneath it and rolled under the armored truck. The driver of the parcel truck got up from his seat and adjusted his right mirror. He then got back in his seat, buckled up and drove off. Several minutes later the carrier comes out of the store, still smiling and swinging the bag gladly as he walked. Once he got about three feet from the truck, he suddenly stopped and walked back into the store. Deuce froze, undoubtedly wondering if the heist should then be aborted or not, but almost immediately, the carrier came back outside with his cap in his hand. He fit it snugly on his head and toddled for the truck and when he reached for the door there was a thump as it unlocked. His hand gripped the handle and pulled the door open and just as he lifted his foot to step in, the carrier saw something fly up from between his legs into the truck. A large bang rang through the truck and the door flew wide open. Deuce rolled from underneath the truck and then there were two more resounding bangs coming from behind the truck. The carrier and everyone around fell to the ground looking around for the source of two shotgun blasts. About the time they noticed the station wagon pulling away, Deuce had entered the truck, took the keys and threw the driver outside. Consequently, just as he had planned, Deuce shot up the feeder road and onto I635. He made it to Luna Road just over 5 minutes later. He turned into the hotel parking lot and slammed on the brakes. The guy who rode with Mario rushed out the car and tried to enter the truck once it had stopped, but Deuce pushed him down as he hurried out of the truck. Fifteen seconds later there was a large explosion inside the truck and Deuce went back inside. They emptied the truck and climbed into the getaway car with Mario yelling as they burned off. There was not a cop in site. The heist was an astounding success. However, as they celebrated, Deuce eyed a familiar blue Corvette in the adjacent parking lot among the cars. Yet, he just rolled over in his seat and stared up at the roof of the car.

They drove all the way to Hurst and rented a motel room. They stayed there well into the night counting and dividing the money. About 12 am, there was a knock on the door. They hurriedly grabbed the money and were stashing it all underneath the bed. At that time, the door flew open and six people dressed in riot gear stormed into the room. There was no time to go after their guns before they were kicked about and roughed up by their assaulters. Each of them were quickly banded with nylon cable ties, stuffed in the back of a police car and hauled away before they knew what was happening.

As the car sped along I183, an alert came over the radio. "Be on the alert...an Irving officer has been assaulted and his cruiser stolen...the assailer was wearing black fatigues and a black ski mask...The suspect is suspected to be a six-foot male –between 200 to 230 pounds." The driver, still wearing the ski mask and fatigues, laughed and adjusted the rearview mirror.

"Hey!" Deuce yelled, "Are you the po-po?" However, the driver didn't answer. They simply exited Esters Road and pulled into a small shopping center. Once they stopped, the driver got out of the car, opened the rear door and quickly slapped a pair of handcuffs on Deuce and popped him on the forehead before tossing a knife on the floor in front of him. While Deuce's newfound crew scuffled for the knife, the driver hopped into a nearby pickup truck and drove away.

Deuce was so upset he didn't wait for them to retrieve the knife. He jumped out of the car and sprinted down the road and into an apartment complex. The other three guys were not far behind him. They all regrouped behind a large dumpster and managed to cut the cable ties off their hands, but couldn't help Deuce with the handcuffs. Mario's guys were yelling at each other, confused about what happened and wondering how they would now get their money.

"Somebody had to be following us, dude," one of them said.

"How they know we had the money?" the other shouted. However, the looks on Deuce and Mario's faces suggested that they were suspicious about the efficiency in which the robbery was carried out, but neither of them said a word.

Later that afternoon, Deuce and Mario met up at Crimson Moon looking for JC, but no one was there, so they called Greg to come and unlock the handcuffs. Deuce was still highly annoyed by the whole ordeal and paced back and forth swearing his revenge. Mario stood there quietly until Deuce began to accuse him as well.

"You did this!" Deuce yelled.

"What?"

"You heard me. Nobody knew where we were taking that truck, but you...and I knew I recognized that car in the parking lot. It was Treasure, wasn't it? ...I know it. ...and I know it was Treasure driving the cop car by the way her ass moved when she walked away from us."

"The two of you...and JC... and them other mutherfuckas in the crew –set me up ...took my mutherfuckin' money. I want my shit!" Deuce yelled. "You hear me? I want my shit!"

Mario and Greg both laughed at him, seeing that Greg had arrived in the middle of Deuce's tirade and allowed them into the club.

Your story is hilarious Deuce," Mario replied. "The Reaper ain't never took no legit money. They only rob drug dealers and drug Lords."

"Well, they must've changed their policy because it was the mutherfuckin' Reaper that took my shit."

Just then JC walked into the room behind them.

"Sit down, Deuce," he said.

"I don't wanna sit down. I want my money," Deuce yelled as they all turned around shocked to see JC.

"I'm not gonna tell ya twice, Deuce." The room was silent as JC strolled over to the bar and grabbed four beers. Greg unlocked Deuce's handcuffs and told him to go ahead and sit down. JC came back and handed each person a beer before he had himself a seat at one of the tables.

"That was your gig yesterday?" JC asked Deuce.

"Yeah."

"That was pretty sweet. How much did you get?"

"...'bout four and a half."

"Hmm, $450,000. I can see why you're upset, but this is why I can't help ya. First, I didn't take your money, so whatever ideas you have of that happening, get it out of your head. ...And – secondly, I don't take money from folks who work hard to get it legitimately. ...I steal dirty money 'cause, you see, the po-po don't care 'bout thieves stealing from thieves; they care 'bout thieves stealing from taxpaying citizens. –You see, you stole from the wrong guy, Deuce, and similarly, someone stole it from you..."

"Spare me the motherfuckin' ethics class," Deuce snapped rather angrily, "Tell me how to get my money back."

"First of all, watch your tone and tell me why the fuck you did it," JC asked, before leaning back in his chair and taking a swig of beer. However, Deuce was suddenly without words and JC noticed the uneasiness the question roused in both him and Mario. "I tell you what, forget why you did it. Tell me this, who authorized it? Who gave either of you permission to go over my head and do something so stupid!" The room was silent. JC took out his gun and slammed it on the table. "This is the kinda thing that irks me with the two of you! You don't fuckin think. I'm glad it was stolen! You know why, because if it wasn't the Feds would be running up in here looking for it, and trust me, they won't let up until somebody goes down, and I be damned if I go to jail behind some pocket money. If I go to jail it's gonna be because I walked away with the whole fucking bank! You hear me?" JC yelled, but Deuce didn't respond. He just walked over to the bar and grabbed a bottle of gin and turned it up until he had consumed nearly a fifth of it.

"I'm 'bouts to go," Deuce said. "I'm tired of this shit."

"...Drop a Grant on the counter, nigga," JC told him. "That shit ain't free." Deuce looked up, shocked that JC was making him pay, and reluctantly reached into his pocket and threw a $100 bill on the counter. "Keep the change," Deuce replied sarcastically and walked out the front door with the bottle in hand.

"You can follow him," JC said to Mario, who likewise, got up and left.

CHAPTER THIRTEEN

The next morning JC was woken up from the annoying beeping of his pager. Beeeep! Beeeep! Beeeep...Beeeep! Beeeep! Beeeep! He grabbed it and looked at the display and it showed, "535537834" or "HE BLESSES" when turned upside down. He picked up the phone and called his mother. The phone rang several times before she answered.

"Hello?"

"Yeah, Momma...you paged me?"

"Yeah boy! Why ain't you answering your phone?"

"It ain't rang."

"Boy, I been trying to reach you since 7 o'clock."

"Why? What's going on?"

"I wanna go to that church you went to last Sunday."

"What?"

"I wanna go to church."

"Momma... Why are you messing with me? What's up?"

"I wanna go to church. I'm already dressed so get on over here and pick me up so I can be there before the preacher-man."

"Momma..."

"Get over here, now. I'm already dressed."

JC hung up the phone and looked at the clock. It was 7:40. He went through his normal morning ritual: showering, shaving and skimming through the closet for an outfit.

His mother paged him two more times before he could get to her. He arrived sometime after 9 a.m. and his mother was waiting for him on the porch when he did. He couldn't believe ol' Mary was so serious about going to church. He had never known her to step foot in a church house unless there was a funeral. However, just as she wished, JC had her there before the preacher-man. In fact, she was there before everybody.

Once the Deacon showed up and opened the door, Mary grabbed her bible and stepped out of the truck.

"Why you still sitting in this truck?" she asked JC.

"I'm 'bout to go back home."

"Oh no, you ain't. You had better get in here, boy."

"Momma!"

"Come on!"

Reluctantly he joined his mother and they walked inside. The deacon then showed them where their Sunday school class would be held and they took a seat and waited for everyone else to arrive. Once class began, JC looked back to see if Tina had arrived but she wasn't there. The Sunday school teacher then asked JC to stand up and read a verse from the Bible, and he did. His mother was excited to be there and could not be happier when asked to recap the lesson. After the class was dismissed, JC went and got a drink of water. Tina still hadn't shown up so he walked back into the sanctuary and had a seat in the front by his mother.

The church service began promptly at 11 o'clock. The congregation sang a few hymns, they took up an offering and the choir sang a few selections. The choir director was overly animated, as usual, stressing this note and that one and when Reverend Liverpool took the pulpit, he sang yet another song before he delivered the message. He was brief with his preaching that day, however, and service was dismissed around 1 o'clock. Then just as they were leaving their seat JC saw Tina and her mother ushering at the church entrance.

"Hey, Mom. I want you to meet somebody," he said.

"Wait a minute... I want to meet the pastor first."

"The Pastor? You just heard him talk for an hour."

"Boy, don't you sass the preacher-man. Now come on here."

JC strolled on up to the altar with his mother. She was so excited she couldn't wait for the person before her to wrap it up. The Sunday school teacher stood at Reverend Liverpool's side the whole time. JC glanced back at Tina, but she still hadn't seen him. He looked up at the Pastor as his mother stepped up and then noticed the table next to them with the words "In remembrance of me" engraved across the front.

"Come on Momma, this is taking too long," he said, but it was too late. His mother had already begun to speak.

"Reverend Liverpool, I sure enjoyed myself today."

"Oh...well good, God sho' is good ain't he?"

"He sho' is. ...This is my son Jonathan," she said as she led him closer to the Pastor.

"How you doing young man," Reverend Liverpool asked, as he reached out to shake JC's hand.

"I'm good," JC replied as he shook the Reverend's outstretched hand.

"He told me about last Sunday's service and I just had to come to see for myself," Mary commented.

"...Really?" Reverend Liverpool replied, "So you liked the

message?"

"Man, I slept through your message," JC responded.

Just then JC's mother smacked him upside the head.

"Momma!" he yelled.

"I told you not to be sassing the preacher-man, didn't I?"

The Pastor and Sunday school teacher laughed.

"I remember you," The Sunday school teacher commented. "He'll be alright."

JC began to grow impatient as the conversation with his mother and Reverend Liverpool seemed to have no lasting purpose. However, when it finally ended, JC and his mother exited down the center aisle. Once they got to the door, Tina's eyes bucked when she saw him. He, appropriately, reached out for her hand but she jumped to hug him. He was shocked, being that she was so reserved around her mother and church folk.

"Momma, this is my girlfriend Tina."

"Hey, baby. How you doing," Mary asked, as they gave each other a big hug.

"I'm doing fine, Ma'am, "Tina replied.

"Wanna meet my momma?"

"Why, sure I do, child." Just then TIna tapped her mother, who was speaking to one of the church members, on the shoulder and she turned around. When Ms. Sanchez's eyes landed on Mary, a series of tears streamed down her face. She then scurried up the step, wiping her tears and straightening her dress. She paused and then grabbed Mary's hand.

"Madam Calderon, It's good to see you," she said.

"I'm Marylyn Cain," Mary replied as she attended to pull her hand free.

"Oh, no. Oh no. I know you," Ms. Sanchez shouted. "I'm Jessica. I was married to Joseph. You remember Joseph don't you?"

Everyone stood around watching her. She was almost hysterical, pulling at Mary's hand and refusing to release it. Tina pulled her mother away and hugged her tightly. "It's ok, Momma. It's ok. Everything's gonna be just fine. ...Come on let's go." JC hurried to help Tina and Ms. Sanchez to the car. As they helped her into the car, JC reached over to fasten her seatbelt and she grabbed his arm violently "I knew there was something familiar about you. You look just like yo' daddy," she said. JC gently removed her hand. "It's gonna be alright, Ms. Sanchez. I promise you." He then shuts the door and walked Tina to the other side of the car. She gives him a hug and then wipes the tears from her face.

"Oh my God, she's getting worse, Jonathan."

"What's wrong with her?"

"She's battling with dementia. –Sometimes she seems to be okay, but... I don't know. I can't really explain."

JC hugs her tightly, "I'll always be here for you. You hear me? Whenever you need me, I'm there and that's a promise."

Tina undoubtedly appreciated that. However, her frown continued to grow and the tears streamed down her face. "I'd better go. ...gotta get Momma her medicine."

"Ok. You want me to come over?"

"No. ...I'll call you." "

Ok."

Tina jumped into the car and kissed her mother on the temple and started the car. JC just stood there as they drove off. His mother had gone back into the church by then, and when he finally found her, she looked as if she had been crying.

"What's wrong Momma?"

"This is why I don't come to church," she snapped. "People

here are crazier than hell."

JC laughed, "That's not nice Momma. She just hadn't had her medication."

As JC was aiding her down the steps, she stopped and looked at him closely. "You call yourself in love with that lil' girl?"

"She's good to me," he replied. "...I like her a lot."

"...Then be good to her. She's got enough problems with that mother of hers; don't be making her life any more complicated than it is."

He didn't respond to her last comment, just walked her to the truck and drove her home. Not much was said on the way. Mary had become a little wired behind the Jessica Sanchez experience and was only interested in getting home and getting a hot cup of coffee.

Once he dropped his mother off he drove to Deuce's house, but he wasn't there so he went to a nearby payphone and paged him. Several minutes later Deuce called him back.

"Yeah..." Deuce said as JC picked up the phone.

"Where you at? –You close to Xavier's?"

"Yeah, I'm at the Ridgewood Stop and Shine getting the car detailed. What's up?"

"...I'll catch up with you in 15 minutes. Wait on me."

"Yeah... I just got here anyway," Deuce replied. "I'll be here."

Deuce smirked as he sat the phone on the hook and went back to watching the ladies rub down his car. The Ridgewood Shop and Shine was the larger of JC's two detail shops. It was located in the northwest corner of Ridgewood Drive and Lake June. It was fully staffed with women; Black women, Mexican women, three white women and one Asian. They all wore form-fitting t-shirts and short shorts to entertain the patrons as they got their vehicles detailed. Deuce was there several times a week, if not to just hang out and flirt with the girls.

When JC arrived he walked up to Deuce and asked him to come inside with him. When they got into the office, JC immediately began to question him.

"What's up with the defiance?"

"...The what?"

"...Defiance! I asked you to see what Mario knows; to see who his contacts are and to let me know what his dealings are with Antonio. I didn't ask you to go out and rob a fuckin' armored truck with him or to go out and bring heat back on us."

"Man you told me to be creative."

"...Creative in getting the info, not in venturing off into your own shit."

"Look, man, I ain't even trying to get into it with you today. What I know is the more he trusts me the more I'm findin' out, and this money thing is where his mind is now. So if you want me to get all the information, you have to allow me to take this thing all the way."

"You know what that means don't you?"

"What?"

"It means I have to look at you like every other two-bit hustler on the street."

"So..."

"So during this process and until you are successful, we ain't friends. If my money is fifty cents short, I will rip you a new ass. – Do what you do. Make your money and get me my information soon."

"A'ight, but once I do this; I want full inclusion in The Reaper."

JC twirled a pen between his fingers while he stared Deuce down. Then he suddenly placed the pen back in the penholder and got up from the desk and approached him.

"If you pull this off we'll vote on adding you."

Deuce squinted and bit his lip after JC's response.

"I need you to get Treasure off my ass and give me an advance," Deuce replied.

"I'll always have eyes on you, Deuce, whether it's Treasure or not. … And you have to fund your own shit. …Do what you do."

"How do I know you won't turn on me later?" Deuce asked.

"I ask myself the same question about you every day."

The two of them shook hands in agreement but Deuce was enraged by JC's words and stormed out the door. JC watched from the window as Deuce jumped into his car and sped down the street. The two of them were now in an area of the game that was foreign to each of them and the outcome could not be foreseen.

CHAPTER FOURTEEN

Three months would pass before any major activity occurred in Pleasant Grove. There were the regular stories of shootings, domestic disputes, and rival gang activity filtering through the news, but nothing of any significance, outside of the large annual fireworks show held in the Lake June Roundabout. However, beyond the marketable interests of television and newspaper reporters, deep in the why in the hell would I go there parts of Dallas, Deuce had quickly gotten lower Pleasant Grove in an uproar. He had begun to sell twice as much product than he had under JC and organized a small team of guys to assist him.

These measly three months had proven profitable for him, but not without routine run-ins with the cops and frequent visits by Antonio and his men. Janice also had a hand in keeping him riled up. After she broke out his windows the first time she returned and broke them out again, and as you may expect, he searched the whole of Dallas for her. However, when he finally found her, he wished he hadn't. She had broken into his house, banged and bruised herself and called the cops. Deuce was, consequently, arrested and taken to jail and when all was said and done, the police found a way to keep him there a whole week. What's more, when he was finally released, his friend Janice had once again disappeared.

Mario's luck was even worse. He spoke to JC a week after the armored truck heist and asked him about the next Reaper meeting. JC was very nonchalant but dubiously advised him that all meetings and activities were postponed due to the Fed heat he and Deuce caused, even though, no Fed had visited him or any of his establishments. Mario, knowing JC, sensed that something was wrong but appropriately walked away making no mention of it.

The following week JC found out that Mario was the second driver he and Deuce spotted that day at Williams Chicken. Furthermore, to make matters even worse, JC was informed that Victor and Mario were trying to make a quick profit off the money Victor was supposed to pay Antonio's mules with. As a result, Antonio had Mario severely beaten and broke both of Victor's arms and of legs. Now, Mario is being made to do Victor's job under the constant threat of losing his life.

It was September 09, 1982 when JC threw Tina's college acceptance party. The two of them had grown considerably closer and he spared no expense in having the first floor of Crimson Moon converted into a giant Christina Sanchez mural. He hired the best graffiti artist in the area to complete the task, and the work was stupendous. The mural could be seen as soon as you entered the door. It seemingly told the story of Tina's life from childhood to present and spanned the walls from the concession stand all the way back around to the exit. Tina loved the mural, and her favorite scene was the one that showed her at Xavier's, covered in flour.

All of their friends were there. The only people who weren't present were Mario and Deuce. JC had the occasion catered by Xavier's on Lake June and hired a local photographer to get a snap of every smile. It was a happy time and the night progressed almost effortlessly. JC gave a brief speech about his experiences with Tina over the previous couple of months and Tina followed him with a short remark about her college acceptance.

Once Tina stepped down from the makeshift stage, Greg climbed upon it and called Sheila up. Tina stepped aside clapping with everyone else as Sheila approached. She was blushing heavily, having no idea of what was about to happen. A slow ballad began to play and Greg grabbed her hand and assisted her onto the stage. Then looking deep into her eyes, he kissed her hand and lowered himself to a knee. Sheila's father rose from his seat but didn't move from his spot. At which time, Greg reached into his pocket and pulled out a small case that exposed a brilliant diamond atop a gold wedding band.

"Sheila, My love," he said softly into the mike. "When I met you, I thought you had the beautifulest eyes I'd ever seen. I fell instantly in love with you and have longed for you ever since. Now, I may not be smooth like JC, or a muscle head like some these other guys, but I am the answer to your dreams, as you are the answer to mine; and I hope you will take me into your heart and have me as your husband. —Ms. Sheila Wilson, what I'm trying to say is will you marry me?"

Sheila was speechless. She stood there looking down at him in astonishment. Greg stood up and looked her in the eyes and repeated the question. "Ms. Sheila Wilson, will you marry me?" Sheila looked over at her parents, and her dad shook his head and began to clap. Everyone joined in, clapping in unison.

Sheila's eyes filled with water and the tears began to fall. Tina, who had also begun to cry, stepped closer and put her hand on Sheila's shoulder. Sheila turned to hug Tina, but then suddenly turned back around and hugged Greg.

"Yes! I'll marry you," she yelled as she buried her head in his chest.

He kissed her on the forehead and she lifted her head and kissed him back. It was a long passionate kiss, one that was equal to that of a wedding kiss. Her parents came up to the stage and hugged their daughter and soon-to-be son in law. JC hugged Tina and then shook hands with Greg and Sheila.

"Wow!" JC said as he took the mike from Greg, "I wasn't expecting this tonight. Is there anyone else who wants to get their proposal on before we turn it back over to the DJ?"

Everyone laughed, but no one else proposed. The gathering went on for several more hours but when Tina's mother got tired, Tina left to take her home.

Xavier patted JC on the shoulder and commented on the walls and the way the occasion turned out. JC laughed joyfully and made note of Greg's surprise proposal. Then Xavier nudged him with a devious looking smile on his face.

"...It don't look like you're too far behind him."

"I'm a whole lot farther behind him. Tina and I... We ain't like that."

"What do you mean, like that?"

"...All that mushy stuff. We cool, know what I mean?"

"Man, any woman who witnesses her girl get married is going to want to follow along and get married too."

"Psst...I have too many things to accomplish before I start thinking 'bout marriage."

"..Like what?"

"...like ...like ...I just got stuff to do."

"A'ight, Mister, better get ya stuff done quick. Ol' girl ain't gone be playing once she gets a good look at Sheila's ring."

"Whatever," JC replied. "...What you got on them chicken wings? They're off the chain fo' real." Xavier laughed and continued on with his conversation.

About that time, the regular club crowd began to come in and most of the people who were there for the special occasion were leaving. However, JC and Xavier went upstairs and played a game of dominoes. They played around, laughing and joking all the way up the stairs to the second floor. Then just as JC sat down and started shuffling the dominoes, Gimme rolled up to the table and nudged him.

"...Guess you next," he said mockingly.

"Nah! Not me," JC shook his head no. "I just got through telling your punk ass cousin 'bout that nonsense. Tina's going to college. That marriage stuff won't be on the menu for another four, five years."

"You won't last another 18 months," Xavier said.

"What you got on it?" JC said. ."

"I got a bill on it," Xavier countered.

"I'll match that $100," Gimme added.

"Oh! Ok," JC replied. "I'm gonna take both of y'all's money...now who got Big-six?"

They all had fun that night hanging out with friends. JC and his crew had all left Crimson Moon by twelve, but most of them were back before daylight the next morning for the meeting. Sync was the first one there. He arrived about 5:30 to review the tapes from the previous day and make sure no one was hiding away in a closet. Everyone else trickled in between six and six-thirty and dallied about as usual. JC sat down and pulled his leather chair up to the big mahogany conference table around seven and called everything to order.

"I know everyone here is wondering why we're here at seven in the morning…and I must admit, it was a spur of the moment decision, but a lil' more variation in the meeting times should prevent situations like the one we had last. Now before I begin, I want everyone who doesn't already know to be aware that Deuce has been given full control and ownership of all the street interests. –He has also been given the task of gathering the information we need about the link between Mario and Antonio. "As you all know, Antonio has been hand and hand with every move we make and the only way this could be remotely possible is if one of us was snitching to him. Now, Gimme and Deuce have provided me with enough information about Mario's activities to convince me that he has had some ill-advised dealings with Antonio and his affiliates. However, no one is to act on it because I want conclusive information about what these dealings were. Until then, avoid contact with both of them, Deuce and Mario, and make sure they stay in the dark about our activities until I decide how we will deal with them. Does anyone have any questions?"

"Yeah," Gimme said as he adjusted himself in his wheelchair. "I know you, Sync and Treasure have a good reason for choosing Deuce, but don't you think that's a lil' too much responsibility for him?"

"Not at all," Sync interjected. "By using Deuce, we keep him distracted …and we minimize the risk associated with losing one of you. Deuce draws a lot of attention to himself, which means he will draw attention away from us, so we benefit whether he gets our information or not."

By the remarks that were made around the table following

Sync's explanation of why they chose Deuce, Gimme and many others agreed that Deuce could handle this task in a way that many could not. Yet, as the conversation continued, JC added, "Deuce has asked that, if he pulls this off, he be included in The Reaper." Everyone laughed at Deuce's arrogance, knowing very well that he lacked the right character for such an opportunity. "I told him we would vote on it," JC continued, and everyone quieted, looking back at him as if they were waiting for the punch line. "I gave my word, so we will vote, but whatever decision you come up with will stand."

"Are you seriously considering including him?" Greg asked.

"I don't know. I thought 'bout it the night I took him to see Antonio, but there was an incident with him and one of Antonio's boys and another incident with him and a broad at Johnnie's. At this point, it goes to be seen...depends on how he does over the next couple of months. We can always use his bank and armored car taking skills."

"For what?" one of them asked. "I mean the brotha's tight on that kind of thing, but that's not what we do."

"Yeah, I know," JC replied, "but you can only get away with what we do for so long. At some point, we will need an exit strategy, so we may have to clean a bank." A few people laughed thinking he was joking.

Then Treasure looked up at JC. "You know a bank is going to bring Fed heat."

"Yeah, I know."

"This is why it has to be done one time and done right."

"Wait a minute," Sync said as he sat up in his seat, "are we really considering this?"

"Maybe," JC smirked.

"...With the right plan and a bankroll big enough to retire on,"

Treasure followed, "I'd be all over it."

"...Done once and leaving with everything!" Gimme shouted as he slapped the table in front of him, "I'd definitely be down with it."

"Shut Y'all asses up," Scratch added, "Who gone help me count that shit?"

Everyone laughed at Scratch's sarcasm and spoke briefly among themselves until JC drew their attention back to their immediate task: the PGA project. He compiled the information they each had gathered and listed the top five obstacles on a blank sheet of paper he called the Master List. Sync laid a blueprint of the Pleasant Grove Apartment Complex on the table and they began to coordinate the order and orientation of events. "You gotta be patient," Sync said a half dozen times while describing their objective.

"Pleasant Grove Apartments are the Fort Knox of the ghetto," Sync said as he assumed his position as The Reaper's Event Coordinator. "No one has ever successfully robbed or raided this place. They're responsible for half of the heroin distribution in the region, and as we stated prior, there are five major concerns with taking PGA: The first and most important factor is that it is under surveillance by the Feds. The second is that it is built on a cul-de-sac and there's only one way in and one way out. Hence, we have to plan this thing backwards so that if anything goes wrong, everyone can get away safely. Now, the whole thing is gonna hinge on how effectively we manage obstacle three: the North and South Sets. ...Be careful not to undermine the fact that these two factions are actually the same gang. As much as they war between each other, they will bond like cement against any outside threat. It is approximately 2,800 of them and only eleven of us with Mario out, so we have to be like Marines –

swift, silent and deadly.

...There's no room for mistakes here. If they find out who hit them they will hunt us down like animals, one by one, so we have to make this look like an accident, and then move the merchandise before anyone realizes that it wasn't. —Five objectives: avoiding the feds, getting in and out, getting around the sets, making it look like an accident and moving the merchandise. We must be inconceivably precise..."

The meeting went well into the day and, as usual, there was catering from Xavier's so they took a break around noon for lunch. By 1:30, they were back to business. This was the first and most intense of three separate meetings that would occur over the next three weeks, each with its own significance. The first meeting was to discuss the first three concerns with taking PGA, the second was to discuss the last two concerns and the third was to tie them all together. However, before that third meeting, there was a false meeting which included Deuce and Mario. In that meeting, JC and Sync discussed a mock plan to take PGA and Deuce and Mario were led to believe that they were part of the action. The two of them left the meeting believing that they would be driving the truck with the money and merchandise from PGA to a secluded area where Xavier would later retrieve it. They seemed as eager to play their part as JC did to keep them in the dark about what they were really doing.

Thursday evening JC left the barbershop groomed to perfection. He was wearing a dark blue suit and a rose-colored shirt. He had the swagger of a celebrity as he approached Betty, dropped her top and sat down in the comfort of her plush leather seats. She cranked right up and hummed soft and low at the turning of his key. He was off to see Tina who was supposed to meet him at the Lake June Roundabout for a romantic dinner around seven o'clock. It was now 6:45 and he had nearly a 15-minute drive to Lake June. He was smiling like a kid waving at people he recognized along the way. He was probably more excited to meet up than Tina was, having not seen her as much as he would have liked to since she had begun her college studies. Once he arrived at the Lake June Roundabout, he drove around the circle until he saw Tina's car. He parked next to it and adjusted his suit and he got out. Still smiling like a kid he walked across the center island looking for Tina. After missing her on his first pass he walked back across. "Are you looking for Ms. Sanchez?" one of the servers asked as they were heading back to Comasca's, an Italian restaurant at the Northeast corner of the roundabout.

"Yes, I am," JC replied with a bit of amazement.

"She went across the island to Pelican Bay."

JC froze in place for half a second. His eyes glossed over and he slowly turned back towards Antonio's restaurant.

"...Are you ok?" The server asked.

"Yeah," JC replied, "...I'm perfect... just perfect."

"Alright then," she said caringly, "You have a great day Mr. JC."

"Yeah, you too," he mumbled.

He then walked back across the island as if each step was on a sheet of thin ice. He had to be wondering why Tina would have left the roundabout without telling him and why, of all places, would she go to Pelican Bay. As he entered the foyer the hostess immediately came from around the counter and said, "Señor Cain, you must follow me." Without a word spoken back, he followed her up the stairs. The room was beautiful. The chandeliers shimmered in the soft lighting and made the peach room feel warm and inviting. Antonio sat on the far side of the room with Tina sitting to his right. She had on a dazzling rose-colored dress that matched JC's shirt. As JC approached the table Antonio stood.

"Hey, Jonathan, my son!" he shouted as he reached over and hugged him. "You having a good day, no? ...Sure you are. I saw Ms. Sanchez outside by herself so I took the liberty to invite her in. Come on, sit down."

Antonio sat JC down next to Tina and then sat across from them. He grabbed his napkin off the table and tucked it into his shirt like a bib. "I took the liberty to order for you since you were late," Antonio continued. "So what you up to, Jonathan," Antonio asked as the waitress placed their dinner on the table. "What? Cat got your tongue? Come on! Tell me what's been going on?" JC was still without words, frozen to his seat staring straight at Antonio.

"Jonathan, what's wrong," Tina asked. "You didn't even say hi."

Antonio looked up from the table where the waitress was serving each of them a half pound of Angus Prime Ribs, a 10-ounce oven-roasted lobster tail, Char-Grilled Chili-Lime Prawns and an assortment of vegetables.

"Jonathan!" Tina shouted.

"Yeah," JC replied, "...I ...I'm sorry. How are you, baby?"

"I'm fine. Why are you acting so strange?"

"I just got caught up in the moment. That's all. I've never seen anything quite like this."

Antonio laughed. "Loosen up, Jonathan. You act like you're having dinner with the mob or something."

"Yeah, Tony's good people," Tina said.

"Tony?" JC snaps.

"Yeah, Tony told me that he was your boss and that you were one of his most promising employees. —Jonathan, he says you closed an important deal for him yesterday that saved him thousands of dollars. Why didn't you tell me?"

"I uh..." JC stammered.

"Jonathan is modest," Antonio interjected. "He does lots of stuff for me. Go ahead and eat. The food's fabulous."

Antonio polished his silverware with his napkin, winked at JC and continued. "A couple of months ago one of my competitors was getting a little too close for comfort and this man... Wow! ...Jonathan and his team made them literally ineffective overnight. They went bankrupt!" Antonio then laughed like he was being tickled by a house full of kids.

"So what exactly do you do, Jonathan?" Tina asked.

"He's my project manager," Antonio answered in place of him "So how's the food, Ms. Sanchez? You like?"

"I like," Tina says with a big smile on her face. "This place is great. The food is great, and you, Tony; you're like a swell ol' grandpa. I love you already. —JC why you lead me on about what you do. I think all of this is great."

"Tina, you don't quite know what's going on here. I think we should leave."

"Come on. We haven't even finished eating. Plus, before you came in Tony and I were talking about the other guys. I told him about how Greg proposed to Sheila and about Sync; always hiding out in that upstairs room watching videos of everything that happens in the club." Tina laughed and Antonio laughed along with her. "We even talked about Deuce..."

"Dos!" Antonio shouted and then rolled back into laughter.

"Sí, Sr. Dos. Los mundos el maniquí más grande!"

"¿ah, usted dice el español?" Antonio replied.

"... un poco."

"Very good!" Antonio replied. "I like this girl, Jonathan. You be careful to keep her safe. It'd be ashamed if something happened to her out there. You know how hard life can be."

"You listen to me..." JC said.

"Yeah?" Antonio replied.

Suddenly, no words were spoken but the tension in the room rose immensely.

"What's going on?" Tina asked.

"This guy is Antonio Ruiz, the leader of the Columbian drug cartel," JC replied. "This restaurant, Pelican Bay, is but one of his expensive fronts used to launder his drug money. He is not my boss and we are not friends."

Tina cowers at his answer and Antonio stood up and clapped. Then leaning over the table he looked JC in the eyes and said, "Now, tell her who you are."

JC looked at him then back at Tina. Antonio chuckles and sits back down and crossed his legs. "Go ahead young stallion. Rile up now."

"I'm Jonathan Cain, your boyfriend..."

"Blah, blah, blah!" Antonio interrupted. "Tell her! Tell her how you are the biggest thief since Jesse James. Tell her how you robbed one of my trucks a week before you met her or tell her how you hit three drug labs just two days after you met. While we're getting acquainted, why don't you tell her what you did yesterday?"

JC squirmed in his seat and Tina panicked. She began to yell and scream and JC was unable to calm her down. She jumped up from her seat and ran down the stairs. Antonio laughed at the top of his lungs and JC could only look. Tina ran out of the restaurant and across the center island to her car. JC ran after her but wasn't able to catch her before she peeled away leaving behind her sweater and the man who loved her. JC threw his jacket to the ground in anger while Antonio looked down from his upstairs window laughing at the two of them.

A picture had been painted in brilliant hues of audacity, greed and lawlessness. Whether it is beautiful or not, depends on its interpretation. Tina interpreted it one way before, but now, under the light of Antonio's Pelican Bay experience, she is unsure of how to interpret it going forward.

Her immediate reaction was shock. After defending his integrity against her friends, who were sure that he was a Lake June gangster, she was now embarrassed. After asking him about his life and him making light of it all, only to find out that he had not been completely honest, she was deeply upset. JC, Antonio, Xavier and even Greg were not who she had imagined them to be. The life that she had come to know and love since meeting them, was not the life she had imagined it to be. She was confused. She didn't know who to believe or what to believe in. She had gone from being distinguished among her peers to being lost among thieves.

THE END OF
LAKE JUNE: LOST AMONG THIEVES, BOOK 1

Keep reading for an excerpt from
The next P.L. Stafford novel

As JC approached the door of Caribbean Nites, Kevin and several other Rastas quickly surrounded him with their guns pointed at him. "We nah won nah trouble," Kevin said. "Why you com 'er now?"

"I just want to speak to Deuce and have a couple of drinks."

"Ya fah'sure ya not 'er fa trouble, Mon?"

"No trouble, Mon," JC replied, mockingly.

"Dat-ah-cool, Mon. Ya Gimme ya guns."

JC slowly reached beneath his shirt and handed him his pistol. Kevin grunted and nudged him in the chest with the barrel of his shotgun. "Both ya' guns, ya bombaclot!"

JC smiled and reached under his shirt and pulled out his second pistol and handed it over. One of the Rastas then frisked him and gave Kevin the signal that he was unarmed.

"We nah won nah trouble, JC. Ya tok and ya drink. Then ya leave."

"Ok, Mon," JC replied.

"We give ya bok ya guns when ya go.

"Cool. Can I go in now? Damn!"

"Yea, Mon! Welcome to da Caribbean Nites Baa 'en gwill. Gwon in and enjoy ya'self, Mon?"

JC walked in with caution, nearly tripping twice on the uneven floors before he found Deuce nestled in the corner wooing a young lady. "Deuce!" JC shouted as he grabbed a chair and took a seat at the table. Deuce looked up at him with amazement.

"Damn, they let anybody up in here now." he replied, as he

pushed the young lady aside.

"Yeah, but at least I'm unarmed."

"Ha! You get a weapon up in here you're good. These boys don't play."

"I see. So how's the food?"

"I like the chicken. The gin ain't half bad either." JC laughed.

"Oh, so gin is a food and not a drink?"

"Gin is vitamin motherfuckin G." JC shook his head and ordered a beer and a plate of Jerk Chicken, per Deuce's recommendation.

They engaged in small talk for over an hour or so before Deuce leaned over to JC and uttered, "Ya boy Mario fucked up."

"How's that?" JC asked.

"He lost a load. Somebody found out what he was carrying and jacked him for the whole truck. Po-po's didn't give a fuck. ...A truck full of meat? They ain't do nothing, but they ain't know there was cocaine packed in that meat either. In fact, you know that truck we hit?"

"Yeah."

"That meat was packed with cocaine, too. Some brotha with a butchery is helping Antonio move his stuff in."

"So how'd he slip up? what happened?"

"I don't know. Probably told somebody something he shouldnt've, trying to do that same shit him and Victor was trying to do."

"So, where he at now?"

"I don't know. He's hiding though. I betcha that shit. Antonio's gone kill his ass this time, but you know something? I don't think that brotha was squealing to Antonio 'bout what Y'all do. Nah.... Antonio don't particularly like him. —All he thinks 'bout is his money."

"...And that ain't all you think 'bout?"

"Hell nawl. Hell, Antonio has snatched my ass too."

"What?" JC shouted.

"Hell yeah. ...told me that you told him that them crack houses was mine and I owed him the $100,000 you owed him. Shit. I hit that motherfuckin' armored truck and then this mutherfucker hits me. Took all my money and told me it was payment towards what I owe him. Ha! What kinda math this motherfucker doing?"

"That's fucked up?"

"Hell yeah, but what you gon' do? That motherfucka's snatching people off the street at will. Surprised he ain't snatched one of y'all and see what you're up to."

"It's worst than that, he got to Tina."

"Tina? That fat hipped broad you all soft behind?"

"Yeah," JC chuckled. "He was all suave with it. ...Had her up in his private dining eating steak and lobster acting like he's a friend of the family. Now, she thinks I'm Al Capone and shit."

"You're worst than Al Capone, Mutherfucker!"

"Shut up," JC replied as he took a swig of his beer and looked up at the Rasta staring at him from across the room. "I should've been more honest with her and let her decide whether she was down or not." He took another swig and then cut his eyes at Deuce. "She's a keeper and I need me a keeper."

"Fool, you're wayyyy too soft behind that broad. ...Talking about what you need. What you need is to stay focus on getting this paper."

"Oh, you're instructing me now, huh?"

"Hell nawl, man. I'm just saying Antonio don't have nothing to gain from fucking with that broad's head other than knowing that it fucks with yours. He knows what we all know. She's your achilles heel. —Dump that broad and get you a throwaway, Man."

"...Like Janice?" JC mocked.

"Awww Man. That's fucked up. You know I got that broad pregnant?"

"You didn't get her pregnant."

"Man, that broad's ballooning like a motherfucka.. She's pregnant, alright. -So, tell me, how'd whats-a-dingy turn out?"

"What the hell is a whats-a-dingy?"

"The thing we did the other day."

"I guess it's cool since the Feds hit it right after we did. Nobody even knows it happened yet."

"I shouldn't have told you that I'd do that job for free. That was a lot of damn money. I bet that old broad that counts your money kept a good $15,000- $20,000 off the top."

JC just laughed at his comment and reached out for a handshake. "Thanks for looking out."

"Yeah, Man. Don't forget our deal," Deuce shouted, referring back to him being voted into The Reaper.

"I won't," JC said as he shook his hand.

LAKE JUNE:
LOST AMONG THIEVES
BOOK TWO

AVAILABLE SEPTEMBER 2018

ABOUT THE AUTHOR

P.L. Stafford is a native of Houston. His earliest writing efforts began in his early teen years and included poems and rap music. By the time he attended high school, he had begun to write articles for the local chapters of S.A.D.A (Students Against Drugs and Alcohol) and S.A.D.D (Students Against Drunk Drivers). It was there that a true affinity for writing was born.

He joined the Marine Corps soon after finishing high school and concurrently attended college achieving bachelor's degrees in Business Administration and Accounting.

While in college, he would become involved in the world of poetry and Spoken Word. This and the innumerable ten and twelve-page essays that paved his way to academic success fueled his desire to take his writing to the next level and his first short story, *Tres Llaves* was born.

Now, after many years of freelance and ghostwriting in the shadows, he has emerged with the first novel under his own name, *Lake June: Lost Among Thieves*.

Currently residing in the Galveston Bay-area, a stone's throw from the sea, he continues to pursue his lifelong dream of being a bestselling author.